Suddenly a gust of wind came from behind and showered her with a sheet of warm rain. A living thing, the blast tore at her hands as she clung to the doorknob with all her might. But as quickly as the wind came, it died down again. She quickly and carefully shut the door. Her entire body shook from the strain and she fought the temptation to sit for a moment. Another blast of wind tore at her, this time from her left side. The black veil peeled away from her head and for a moment was suspended in the air. Only the pins discreetly hidden in the black folds kept the piece of cloth in place. A flash of lightning split the sky. A shiver ran through Margaret like a cold finger up her spine.

She tried to concentrate on finding the pathway . . .

For Joan
Who always has been and will always
be the wind . . .

About the Author

Kris Bruyer lives in Spokane Washington with her partner, four cats and a dog. Currently studying law, she plans to fight for the rights of women and children.

BY KRIS BRUYER

THE NAIAD PRESS, INC.
1995

Printed in the United States of America on acid-free paper
First Edition

Edited by Christine Cassidy
Cover design by Bonnie Liss (Phoenix Graphics)
Typeset by Sandi Stancil

Library of Congress Cataloging-in-Publication Data

Bruyer, Kris, 1962–
   Whispers / by Kris Bruyer.
      p.   cm.
   ISBN 1-56280-082-5
   I. Title.
PS3552.R846W45   1995
813'.54—dc20   94-43990
                                               CIP

PROLOGUE

Astoria, Oregon
July 21, 1896

Sister Mary Margaret waited in the stillness of her cell. The candles and oil lamps had long since been blown out. Most of the other women were already asleep. From her window, she watched as the tempest blew against the stoic walls of the convent. Her prison for the past four years. And refuge.

The wind pummeled the trees, and the weaker, dead branches snapped. Her attentive gaze watched the grounds. Nothing. For a single moment she allowed herself to stare at the raging sea.

She reasoned that God must be angry with her; she could not escape it. His wrath loomed everywhere. From behind the veil that she had grown accustomed to, she had seen it in the gloomy corners of the hallways as she walked silently, shoulder to shoulder with Sister Scholastica, to morning vespers and mass. She heard it in Father McClaron's morning sermon. She smelled it in the ocean winds that blew through the rose garden. She knew that He knew. She didn't care.

Quickly, she dismissed her thoughts and turned her attention back to the grounds. She felt as if the signal would never be given, that she would have to wait another four years before she could be free.

From the corner of her eye she caught a glimpse of something moving in the blackness. Her heart raced. Could it be? Unconsciously, she held her breath. Nothing. And then, yes, there it was again. A flash of lightning lit the grounds for a single moment. Her heart beat faster and a smile touched her lips. She saw, from her window three stories up, the one she had been waiting for. She started to wave and then scolded herself. This was the time for speed. And extreme silence.

The only sound in her cell was the slight rustling of her habit. She would not allow the heels of her shoes to touch the floor. An eerie silence enveloped the abbey like a shroud. In the darkness she found her meager belongings — her mother's rosary and a tiny Franciscan cross given to her on the day she took her vows. She had taken precautions earlier to oil the hinges of her door. There would be no sound of her leaving.

Once in the narrow hallway, she could hear the sounds of women snoring. A whimper came from behind Sister Dolorosa's door.

By the time Sister Mary Margaret reached the wide staircase her wimple was soaked with perspiration. She glanced back over her shoulder before she dared the stairs. She imagined the squeaking that would reverberate throughout every silent corner of the convent. From within she heard a voice screaming for her to run, just run. Yet another cautioned her and guided her, step by agonizing step. After what felt like an eternity she stood on the first landing with what looked like a mile to go.

At the bottom of the last set of stairs she allowed herself to breathe. Her muscles trembled and her head throbbed. The last obstacle stood in front of her. Two huge and heavy doors opened out into the front garden that faced the sea. It would be a challenge to keep the doors from slamming open with the great gusts of wind.

Margaret shook out the knots in her arms before she approached the doors. From inside her scapula she pulled out the key. The key she had been trusted with for the past three years. With her finger she found the keyhole and slid the heavy brass key home. A soft click. She had managed to unlock the door to her freedom. She allowed herself a smile, then pressed her body against the door and listened. She decided to wait until there was a lull in the storm.

Her patience was well rewarded for within a few moments she was opening the heavy door. She would have to be quick.

Suddenly a gust of wind came from behind and showered her with a sheet of warm rain. A living thing, the blast tore at her hands as she clung to the doorknob with all her might. But as quickly as the wind came, it died down again. She quickly and carefully shut the door. Her entire body shook from the strain and she fought the temptation to sit for a moment. Another blast of wind tore at her, this time from her left side. The black veil peeled away from her head and for a moment was suspended in the air. Only the pins discreetly hidden in the black folds kept the piece of cloth in place. A flash of lightning split the sky. A shiver ran through Margaret like a cold finger up her spine.

She tried to concentrate on finding the pathway to the wall. The rain weighed down her black wool garments and she felt as though she would drown in her very clothes. Her feet began to hurt in the tight lace-up shoes, a size smaller than her foot. From the beginning, she was told that it was a sacred thing to suffer as the Lord did. She should be happy that she could give something to the souls in purgatory. Sacrifice, Sister, sacrifice. That was all she heard when she had complained for the first few months, but she had learned to live with the pain. She had learned to live like the saints had. She ate one simple meal each day. She slept in a cell that demanded self-sacrifice. She bathed herself each morning, the wash basin half-filled the night before and often times crusted with ice by morning.

She learned the simple prayers. She learned to kneel before the Mother Superior and confess her transgressions. She tried hard to accept the shame in her reason for being there. She learned to swallow her hate for her father. In the four years she had lived there, she had learned that love could conquer all things, and this was the thought that drove her on in the blackness.

At last she stood with her back against the wall. She was free. Lightning ripped across the sky and a loud clap of thunder filled the night air. She loved the sea and the vitality of the storm. She had denied herself for three years and now her soul longed to feel the salty spray of the sea as it crashed against the rocks. With the wind blowing so harshly she would have to be careful if she took the path that ran along the cliff overlooking the sea. But, she cautioned herself, she must waste no time in getting there. Someone in the darkness waited for her, perhaps impatiently.

Ignoring the danger, she walked the muddy trail. She felt like a child again. She took her shoes off and threw them out into the night. She banished the painful memories and smiled. Ahead, a shape waited for her. She hurried toward the far point of the wall. She imagined the feel of arms around her, the security. Since her arrival at the convent at age seventeen, a bitter and angry woman, she had never known the touch of another. Nuns were not permitted to touch one another.

At the far point of the wall, she paused. The rain beat on her face — the wind had changed directions. Another slash of lightning hit and she saw the figure standing at the designated meeting place, just outside the forest. Her lover was almost close enough to call to.

"Margaret."

"Here. I am here," she called into the wind, into the blinding rain.

Some believed that Sister Mary Margaret slipped from the edge of the cliff that night, while others believed that she committed suicide. No one, however, suspected what really happened that night. One supposes that Margaret did not, could not have heard the person who appeared out of the blackness behind her. Or that she could have ever anticipated what was to happen next, but it was over in a matter of seconds. Two hands and one great shove sent her plummeting over the edge of the high cliff. Her torn body was found the next morning by a young mute boy who came to the convent every day to chop wood for the mighty stove in the convent kitchen.

In the end, the church buried Sister Mary Margaret on the convent grounds along with many of the other nuns that died the following night in the fire. She was buried with her given name engraved on her tombstone: Sister Mary Margaret Winslow. No one knew what she was doing outside the convent that night and no one knew the truth behind her death, save one person who never came forward.

CHAPTER ONE

Portland, Oregon
Summer, 1994

Ashley woke with a start. Slowly her eyes adjusted to the darkness that filled her room. She shivered involuntarily. The dream felt so real. Searching for every detail, she replayed the dream in her mind a second time.

It had been raining, and she was inside a mansion that overlooked the sea. She could remember every detail of the room. There on a great desk lay several papers that appeared to be drawn up for legal matters. The entire room was lined with thousands of books on every subject, but mostly on the occult. The room was lit with oil lamps. Behind the desk sat a man with white hair, mustache and beard. He seemed out of place, and she thought it odd that she should dream about another time. His dress and mannerisms dated from the late 1800s.

The man looked angry and his presence filled the room with a blustery coldness. He was a man who obviously caused fear in others. And a man who thrilled at that fear, devouring it. He clearly trusted no one and cared very little about anyone. Ashley watched him from behind what looked like the folds of a curtain.

Suddenly the door to the study opened, bringing with it a whoosh of air that trembled the flame on his lone candle. The man started, as if unaccustomed to sudden interruptions. He started to rise from his seat.

"What is the meaning of this," he barked. Ashley looked in the direction of the door, but the person was lost in the shadows. The man was angry. "Well?"

"Margaret is dead," the voice from the shadows accused. The voice had no gender. It was monotone, empty of emotion.

"What in the name of God are you talking about," he demanded, squinting toward the door.

"Margaret is dead," the voice repeated. There followed a long silence broken only by the rustle of clothes. And then, quite unexpectedly, a shot rang out in the night. The man's steel blue eyes widened a bit before he fell back into his chair. From his forehead, a thin trickle of blood ran down the side of his nose and into the white mustache.

Ashley screamed so loudly that she thought the entire household would wake up, but to her surprise the only sound she had made was a whimpering when she woke from the dream.

Quickly, she whipped off the covers and turned on her bedside lamp. The shadows in the large bedroom retreated to the hidden corners where light never fully penetrated. This was not the first time she had dreamed so vividly, nor was it the first time she had had this dream in particular.

She checked her clock. It was five-thirty in the morning. She went into the living room and debated calling her friend Emily, who could make her feel better, less tense.

As Ashley was about to give up the idea to call anyone this early in the morning, the phone rang, shattering the silence in the apartment. Ashley jumped, then scolded herself for being so easily startled. "Hello, Emily," she said, knowing.

"Hiya, kid. Bad dream again, huh," Emily asked, her voice a comfort.

Ashley nodded. A gentle, warm feeling turned in her stomach. No matter how she explained it away she still loved Emily, though it had changed its face many times since they had split up and walked their own ways. "Yeah. I was just thinking about calling you," she said.

A soft laughter came over the phone. "But you changed your mind. I can read you like a book."

Ashley shrugged. "I suppose."

"Was it the same dream as before?" Emily asked, her words shadowed with concern.

"Exactly." Ashley yawned.

"Stop by today on the way to work. I want to read your aura," Emily said. It was the same each time they spoke of the dream, and her aura was the same each time she saw Emily afterwards. She wasn't sure why Emily was so concerned, but she humored her. Ashley was about to beg off when Emily said, "Never mind, I know you're dedicated to your work. I'll close down early here and be at the bookstore a little after five. Kisses to Patricia. 'Bye."

The phone went dead before Ashley could get a word in. She smiled to herself and the world looked less terrifying. Emily had always been a positive part of her life. Since grade school the two had been good friends, then lovers through high school and college, and now, back to good friends. Some things never change, Ashley thought as she put the phone back in the cradle. Again the dream tried to invade her thoughts, but she felt stronger since she had spoken to Emily and dismissed it for now.

CHAPTER TWO

Patricia already had the OPEN sign hanging on the door when Ashley arrived at the bookstore. The warm summer air whirled in behind her as she came in off the street. In her usual flamboyant manner Patricia was dressed in hot yellows and light spandex pants that hugged her slightly heavy frame. Her teased red hair looked almost like a flame dotting an *i*.

"There you are, dear," Patricia said, looking up over her reading glasses. She was smiling.

Ashley greeted her quickly. "Morning, Mother." Patricia went back to her book and Ashley ran up the spiral staircase to the office. She dropped her bag, checked her e-mail and, feeling much more composed than when she first walked in, went back to the main floor.

"New books, doll." Patricia pointed one long, ruby red fingernail at several cardboard boxes on top of the counter.

"Great." Ashley smiled. The part she loved best about owning a bookstore, was getting to read the first copy out.

She pulled one of the new hardcovers from a box. *Spiritualism in the Nineties* was written by someone named Catherine Briggston-Paulson.

Ashley flipped the book over to get a look at the author. To her surprise, the woman was young. Most of the people who wrote about the occult were older women. The occasional male author seemed to write about the darker occult subjects. But this woman had an innocent look in her eyes. Ashley inexplicably trusted her immediately.

"She's local." Patricia broke into Ashley's thoughts. "Young, isn't she?"

Ashley nodded and put the book down on the glass case. "Emily is coming over later today. She's going to read my aura."

Patricia raised an eyebrow. "You must've had that dream again. That's the only time she ever wants to read anyone's aura. You know, she wanted to read mine the other day? And I didn't even tell her I had a dream."

Ashley shrugged. "It's true. Emily knows things. She's very powerful."

Patricia nodded. "So am I and so are you, whether or not you care to admit it."

Her mother always said she had the most powerful gift of all the Windlow women. Not even grandmother had such talent. Ashley knew full well that if her mother got off on the topic, they'd be at it again for at least an hour.

"Mother, I'm aware of what I have, but I choose not to use them. I don't understand what's wrong with that. Let's just drop it, shall we."

Patricia, hating not to get the last word in, said to her daughter's back, "Well, I always thought that if you got it, use it. Nothing wrong with that either. Look at Emily, she's made quite a name for herself reading the cards and other things."

Ashley ignored her and kept her back to Patricia. It was an inescapable war and one she didn't wish to get into.

The day dragged on until right before closing. Ashley figured she must have helped at least a dozen customers at the last minute. Shortly after five, Emily made her grand appearance.

"Well, Emily," Patricia said, hugging her. They always embraced even if they had just seen each other the day before. It had become a ritual, and to break a ritual would mean certain bad luck for both of them. Ashley waited and yawned as she watched them carrying on like two long-lost sisters.

When they started off onto some bizarre topic, Ashley figured it was time to break in, but Emily beat her to it. "Now, I hear you've got this wonderful author coming to sign her books," Emily asked as she plucked the Briggston-Paulson book off the shelf.

This took Ashley by surprise. Her mother had a habit of inviting authors to sign their books or give a reading in the store's basement without telling her daughter before she made the arrangements. This was one of those times. Ashley steeled herself. "Mother, you did it again. Why didn't you tell me you set up a signing?"

Patricia turned and blinked uncertainly as though she were trying to remember something. Finally, she said, "Didn't I tell you, dear? She's coming here next week. Her mother called, and well, it seemed like the thing to do. Besides, dear, we could use the sales."

Ashley held up her hand. "I'm not upset about having authors in to sign their books. I'm upset that you choose not to tell me until the week before it happens. Did you do the fliers? Damn it, mother, I'm a full partner in this store. I should be told."

A stern look crossed Patricia's face. "Don't curse at me. And yes, I took the fliers to be photocopied."

Emily chimed in, "It does make your aura awfully bleak, Ashley."

Ashley felt attacked from all sides. "I don't give a damn about my aura."

"I'm sorry." Concern written in her eyes, Patricia approached her daughter. "What's wrong, honey? You're normally not like this. So —" She hesitated as though searching for the right word — "angry."

Ashley shrugged. "I don't know. I haven't been sleeping very well lately. I guess I must be tired." Emily put her arm around her friend and said reassuringly to Patricia, "I know what's wrong. Ashley, come and have dinner with me tonight. We'll talk."

CHAPTER THREE

Emily opened the door for Ashley and the two walked into the quiet Chinese restaurant. They were seated almost immediately in a dark booth in the far corner next to the wall.

Emily made her usual observations of the place. "Dark and dreary. My kinda place." Ashley smiled slightly but said nothing as Emily dug through her purse — the one Ashley had said was the size of an airline carry-on. "Ah-hah!" She pulled out a dark bottle of capsules and pushed it toward Ashley.

"What's this?" she asked, opening the jar.

"My secret 'bring your spirits up' concoction. Take one every day until you feel better."

Ashley grinned. "It looks like a vitamin E pill to me."

Emily scowled at her and teased, "Ashley, I'm crushed. I worked all year to come up with this concoction and you have the gall to say it's a vitamin E pill. That's it, the relationship is over. Give me my pills back and I'll go to that table over there where I know I'm wanted."

Ashley laughed aloud. "All right, I'll take your special concoction."

Emily patted her hand. "I always knew you appreciated me."

Ashley swallowed the pill and mumbled, "I hope it doesn't poison me." Emily slapped her hand playfully and laughed.

When her plate of almond chicken arrived, Emily began to pry. She knew that Ashley was never one to give up information to anyone. That was just one of the reasons they broke up.

Emily still longed for a companion who could stand her flamboyant ways, her eccentricities, her two cats, her zest for the unknown and her incorrigible curiosity. Although Ashley was the one she loved, Emily kept that love close to her heart. There were too many psychics in the world, and she feared discovery of her most vulnerable secrets. Even as she sat across the table from the handsome strawberry blonde, she could feel her heart beat with wanting.

"Tell me what's bothering you," she began slowly.

Ashley shrugged. "I think that it might be the dreams. I seem to be having them more and more often lately."

"Are they more intense or longer?"

Ashley nodded. "Both, actually."

"So much so that it seems you're right there in them?"

Ashley nodded again and took a bite of her special chow mein.

"Well, what does it feel like exactly," Emily prodded, frowning in concentration.

Ashley looked her in the eyes. "It feels like I'm being sucked out of my body. Like if I stay too long in the dream, I'll simply cease to be in this world. Does that make sense?"

It made perfect sense to Emily. "Does it feel like when you're a medium in a seance? You know, that kind of pulling sensation?"

Ashley frowned. "No, it feels more like a tearing. Like somebody is trying to remove me forever from my body. I've never felt this before, even when I did do seances many moons ago."

Emily became alarmed and the hair on her arms stood up. "This is not normal, kid, not normal at all. I remember once I felt that way when I was trying to call up Mrs. Talbot's late husband — you know her, the rich old broad with the blue hair. She still won't admit that she comes to see me once a week, religiously."

Ashley held up her hand before Emily could catch another breath. "Whoa, you're getting way out there, Emily. I didn't tell you this because I wanted to hear about your rich clients and their bizarre behaviors. I told you because I'm really scared."

Emily smiled. "Listen, babe, the best advice that I can give you is to take control of your dreams. It seems to me like the past is calling on the future and someone is trying desperately to tell you something. Didn't Patricia say that you're not the first in your family to experience this?"

"For as long as she can remember, the gift, as she calls it, and the dreams have been passed down to the second daughter of the second daughter."

Emily shuddered as though she had eaten a lemon. "At least it's not the seventh daughter of the seventh daughter. That would be a real goocher. Listen, let me read your cards."

Ashley took a quick look around the restaurant. "Here?"

Emily reached into her purse.

"No, no way. If you insist on doing these strange things, you can come to my apartment and do it. But not here." Ashley was determined.

Emily began to protest, but realized the futility of it. After reading their fortune cookies and paying the check, they headed for Ashley's.

At the kitchen table, with the cards spread out in front of her, Emily tried to concentrate but found her mind wandering. She imagined Ashley moving around in the half-light of the bedroom they used to share. She could nearly feel her touch, and she hungered for those things that were now forbidden to her. Some things, she thought, truly were more desirable when they were forbidden. She rose from the table where the cards were still spread like silent omens.

Ashley had decided to busy herself with getting coffee. The automatic drip pot was steaming in the corner of the large counter top. She didn't hear

Emily come up behind her, but rather felt arms around her waist. It seemed that was where they always belonged. It had been a long time since she had felt the old familiar touch she had grown accustomed to after all those years. A small part of her resisted as the rest of her gave in.

Emily was the first person ever to touch her and there had been no one else since then. After Emily parted quietly on that winter day almost a year and a half ago, Ashley had devoted herself to the store. In the beginning, it felt as if nothing would be the same again, then slowly she began to change. She got used to sleeping alone again. She got used to the emptiness of the apartment that was once light with laughter. And now here she was with Emily's arms around her. It was almost as if Emily had never left.

Ashley turned and their lips touched for what was like an eternity. It felt somehow different. There was no electricity that waved through her body like before. Somehow the moment felt empty.

Emily must have felt the same for she pulled away slowly and, smiling, touched Ashley's face. "It feels funny. The vibes aren't right or something. I think I should go ahead and shove off. God knows Lady Jane and Prince Edward are probably going mad with my being gone this long." Emily scooped up the cards from the table. Her hands were trembling.

As they went to the door, Ashley fought the urge to call her back, but she knew that the second time would be the same as the first. Destiny had planned for them to be undying friends, and that was all. Ashley felt a faded pain pass through her heart as she watched Emily go out the door.

CHAPTER FOUR

On the morning of the signing, Patricia had a 'so tell me all about it' look on her face when she came barging into the office. Ashley was deep into the account books and didn't want to be disturbed, but she knew better than to ignore her, especially when they'd hardly seen each other in the past week. From experience, she knew that her mother wouldn't go away but would become such a nuisance that she would end up telling her anyway. Ashley read the look of disappointment on her mother's face.

"Nothing's happening," Patricia stated, her shoulders slumping a bit.

"Mother, it really is none of your business, but no, Emily and I are friends. Like always. I would like to think that you would've accepted that by now."

Patricia puckered her brightly painted lips. "I know that it's none of my affair, but I sure like Emily and if you're going to be, well, what you are, then I'd prefer to see you with someone really special like her."

Ashley sighed and put her reading glasses down on the open ledger book. Patricia smiled while her thoughts danced. She had always loved Emily like a daughter and it almost broke her heart when Ashley and Emily split the sheets. She told Ashley that it was as hard on her as if Ashley had married and divorced.

Ashley turned to her mother. "It couldn't be that she is so much like you, could it? Really, Mother, when I find someone I care about I'm sure you'll be just thrilled. But can we just drop it for now? I've got a hundred things to do."

Patricia dropped her purse in a locked file drawer. She sighed audibly. "I'm sorry, honey. Now, about the other point of business. It would be nice if you showed your face downstairs when Catherine comes in for the signing. I would like to show off my daughter so Catherine can tell her mother that I didn't raise such a God-awful child."

Ashley nodded. "I'll be down in a while. I have some things to do."

Ashley found her thoughts wandering. She wondered if she'd ever met this Catherine

Briggston-Paulson. Probably not. She would have remembered the name. Even though Portland was a large city, it had many attributes of a small town.

Ashley and her sister had gone to the public schools, and she had met Emily in ninth grade. She was the most bizarre person, other than her mother, she had ever seen. At first Ashley didn't care for her much, but like all things that grow on a person, Emily became irreplaceable.

Ashley smiled. She was grateful that her mother was the way she was. She had taught Ashley not to look down on the world the way so many people did, and that things of real value cannot be taken away or bought.

She wondered what Catherine Briggston-Paulson was like and her curiosity was almost enough for her to climb down the stairs to meet this woman. She remembered the picture on the back of the book and something deep inside of her stirred. "Why the hell not," she asked herself, dropping her glasses onto the stack of ledger books and bills.

Patricia had set up the signing table off to one side, opposite the glass counter where the cash register stood. The table was piled with books by the author. Ashley was surprised to see the entire store swamped with people. They had only been open for fifteen minutes.

She was not surprised to see Emily in the thick of it all, trying to get to the young woman who sat writing on the inside of one of her books. Ashley had to forge herself a small path to get to the counter. "I didn't know that the store would be this crowded, you should have come up to get me," she said apologetically.

Her mother was grinning from ear to ear and brushed off the apology. "She's bringing in the crowds. I knew she would."

Ashley nodded. "It's a good book, even for those of us who don't dwell in spiritualism."

Patricia gasped, looking shocked. "You read her book?"

"Of course, Mother. You know that I read all of the new books that come in."

"When it gets slow I'll introduce you. She's a very interesting woman. I think you'll like her. She seems down to earth, though I can't say that much about her mother," Patricia said.

At that moment, the dark-haired woman behind the table looked up and caught Ashley's eye. Ashley was riveted. Catherine smiled at her and went back to signing her books, but Ashley kept staring at her. It wasn't until Emily came around the counter and spoke to her that she pulled out of her thoughts.

"Attractive, isn't she? But alas, spoken for." Emily sighed. Ashley felt invaded. Sometimes she hated it when Emily could see through her. "Come on, Ash, it's not like you don't wear your heart on your sleeve most of the time," Emily said, her brows raised.

A strange look on her face, Patricia looked at Catherine and then at her daughter.

Ashley avoided the main floor for the remainder of the day and hid back in the office mulling over the finances. She was looking over the catalog of selected items when Emily appeared.

"Sorry," she said as she pulled a chair near the ancient roll-top desk.

"For what?" Ashley asked, concentrating on the page in front of her.

Emily brushed the hair back from Ashley's face. "I didn't mean to be flippant. I didn't know. And I guess I'm sorry about last week too. Some things are just hard to let go of." For the first time, Emily's smile was weak.

Ashley sighed. "We've just got to let go of it. I guess."

"Hey," Emily said brightly. "Pat wants you to come down and meet her newest fascination." Ashley closed the catalog and placed it back with the others on the shelf, then followed Emily down the staircase.

Catherine and Patricia were deep in conversation. Ashley tried to avoid looking at Catherine until they were introduced.

The woman had deep blue eyes with a hint of melancholy that Ashley found sensuous. She fought the urge to lose herself in them and pulled her gaze away.

Catherine was nothing like Ashley feared she would be. She was warm and sensitive, and after a few minutes, Ashley was ready to propose marriage.

Later that week, Patricia invited Catherine, Emily and Ashley for dinner. For the entire day, Ashley hoped that neither Patricia nor Emily would do anything to embarrass her in front of Catherine. She herself was afraid of doing anything that would make Catherine think she came from an odd family. She should have known better.

Dinner went smoothly, but during dessert everything went downhill when Patricia turned the conversation to one of her many obsessions: the family history of the second daughter. Ashley was absolutely mortified.

"There's a dream that I had, and my mother before me," Patricia began. "When my great-grandmother began having it on her fifteenth birthday, it was merely a dream. That was when she discovered that with the dream came the gift. Each recurring dream, from that time on, was slightly different and yet tied together somehow. It's been the same through the years, but the dream seems to get more and more demanding, more real, if you understand. Ashley seems to have the worst one out of all of us."

All eyes turned to Ashley and she knew that she was blushing. She cleared her throat and struggled with her emotions. She was not one to give in to embarrassment or anger, but tonight she was tempted. After a long silence, she said, "If you'll excuse me, I think that I need to take a walk." She glared at her mother and left the table. "Wonder what's the matter with her," she heard Emily ask as the door swung shut.

"She's been awfully moody lately," Patricia said, touching her napkin to her lips.

Catherine, feeling uncomfortable in the embarrassment she knew Ashley must feel, excused herself as well and left the room to try and catch up with Ashley. She caught her as she was swinging the door closed on the back porch.

A few minutes later, Ashley heard footsteps behind her.

"Ashley," a voice called out into the silent summer night. Ashley turned and stiffened slightly. It was Catherine. "May I join you?" she asked shyly.

Ashley smiled. "Sure, as long as you promise not to talk about anything out of the ordinary."

Catherine held up her hand. "I promise."

Ashley led the way down the path toward the wide ocean. Catherine fell in step with her as they walked in the brightness of the full moon.

"It's been a long time since I've been to the beach," Catherine said. "I like the sea air on my face." She closed her eyes and breathed deeply. "It's a wonderful feeling." They walked along in silence.

"I read your book," Ashley finally said, trying to break the awkwardness that had built up between them.

Catherine smiled. "I thought that you didn't want to talk about that kind of stuff."

Ashley shrugged and decided to come clean. "I . . . I don't care for the silence. I never could abide the silence. Besides, I'd like to get to know you better."

Catherine pulled her long, dark hair away from her face and looked intently at Ashley. Ashley wondered if Catherine found her attractive. Catherine seemed mesmerized and kept staring at her. She could not put a name to her attraction as she had never felt this way before with anyone. A smile touched her lips.

"Your mother is an interesting person. I like her," Catherine said finally.

Ashley stooped to pick up a shell that glistened in the light of the moon. She shook the sand away from it. It was a half of a shell in which a clam had lived at one time.

"What do you have there?" she heard Catherine ask.

She wasn't sure if the touch was accidental, but it engulfed her and she was grateful that Catherine could not see her blushing in the darkness. She dropped the shell on the beach and acted like she had meant to do so. "My mother is a strange mixture all right. Sometimes she embarrasses me so bad that I just want to be a crustacean and crawl into a shell," Ashley said as she moved closer to the shoreline.

Catherine followed her and said, "Well, I'm glad that you're not a crustacean."

Ashley laughed and flung a pebble out into the water. "I suppose we'd better head back, otherwise Emily will be out here wondering what we're doing." She grinned, enjoying the private joke.

Then Catherine said rather seriously, "Is Emily your lover?"

Ashley could have fallen over — or worse. There was no escaping the reality of the question. She stopped and looked at Catherine. "No."

Catherine nodded slowly and smiled sheepishly, as if embarrassed at her boldness. "I'm sorry. That was . . . I don't know where that came from. I guess I was curious. Emily and I had quite a long conversation the other day about her sexuality —"

"And so you presumed that because I was her friend there must be something going on between us?"

"No. Actually, I see the way that you look at each other. Look, I'm sorry I brought it up."

Ashley sighed. "It's okay. Don't worry about it. So tell me something about yourself that no one in my family knows."

Catherine was quiet for a while, then said, "I left the convent a year ago today." She laughed as though she shouldn't have made this revelation. She seemed nervous mentioning her past. Ashley supposed people tended to look at her differently when they discovered she had lived in a convent. They probably all asked the usual questions and Catherine no doubt dreaded answering them.

"Why are you laughing?" Ashley asked as she picked another shell out of the sand.

Catherine shrugged. "I get the funniest looks from people sometimes when I tell them that. There aren't many Episcopalian nuns these days."

Ashley tossed the shell out into the yawning blackness of the ocean. "I don't think it's so unusual." She sensed Catherine's fear and added, "Don't worry, I won't ask you any stupid questions."

"Thank you," she said, smiling.

At the bottom of the steps to the house, Catherine suddenly stooped and plucked a shell up off the ground. This time Ashley intentionally touched her hand softly. As she lifted the shell to the light, Catherine trembled slightly. Ashley could feel Catherine's breath on her cheek as they examined the shell. It looked just like the shell she had picked up earlier. The edge was ragged and there was an iridescent pink spot inside. Catherine seemed amazed. The look in her eyes made Ashley kiss her softly. She was certain that Catherine had returned the kiss, but she pulled away suddenly.

"I'm not . . . like that," she said and without another word went into the house.

Stunned, Ashley was left holding a half of a clamshell and cursing herself for thinking with her heart.

CHAPTER FIVE

A few weeks passed. Labor Day came and went quietly. Ashley had not seen Catherine since the night on the beach and figured that she never would again. She had made a bad mistake and though she wished to forget the whole incident and move on, she found herself thinking about Catherine at every quiet moment she had. Several times she was tempted to talk to Emily about her, but Emily and Patricia were apparently socializing with Catherine, and Ashley didn't want to answer the questions she might see in Emily's eyes.

It wasn't until Emily came into the store at closing time one evening that Catherine's name came up in conversation. Ashley was at the top of the ladder shelving some books when Emily, her face flushed, swirled in with the summer night air.

"Where's Pat," she asked excitedly.

Ashley pointed up the stairs and asked, "Why?"

Emily motioned for her to come down the ladder. She had a letter in her hand. "You're not going to believe this. Not in a million years," she said before Ashley was halfway down.

"Well, what is it," Ashley asked, grabbing for the paper.

Emily yanked the letter away, holding it out of reach. "Listen to this. 'Dear Madame Mistorie,' " she read, " 'A few weeks ago I made a trip into the city to find someone who could help us come to grips with a certain problem my wife and I are having with some friends from the other side. Someone mentioned that you are the best psychic in the business and I came by to see you, but found your store closed for the day. I hope that this letter reaches you as we are desperate at this point for any solution to our problem. We will pay your expenses to and from Astoria as well as any expenses accrued there. We are willing to pay you generously for your time and effort in this matter. If you are interested please call the number below. Sincerely, blah-blah.' " Emily's eyes sparkled with amusement.

Ashley frowned. "Probably some nut case. God knows you attract a lot of them, Madame Mistorie."

Emily, clearly hurt, puckered her lips. "I beg your pardon, but I think that the people in my life are very . . . well, okay, so you and Catherine are my only normal friends." Ashley glanced away as Emily went on, "It's legitimate. I called the number and spoke with the guy who wrote the letter. It seems that he and his wife sunk every last penny they had into this huge house that sits overlooking the ocean. They intended to open a bed-and-breakfast of some sort when they ran into a few problems not of this world."

Ashley shrugged. "So what does that have to do with you?"

Emily tossed the letter onto the glass case. "Sometimes I swear you're dense. They want a team of psychics to come into the house and see if they can set the spirits to rest. It sounds like a challenge to me. And I was wondering if you'd be interested."

Ashley said she would have to think about it and left Emily to consult with Patricia.

That night Ashley dreamed in vivid colors. Every word, every movement and every thought were as clear as if she were standing right there.

There was a fruit cellar behind the same mansion that had plagued so many of her dreams. Night had fallen and the stars twinkled in the clear sky. A touch of autumn chilled the night air with its breath. The moon lit up the doors to the fruit cellar which was usually locked from the outside. But on this night, the bar was laid aside and one of the doors was flung open. Ashley could hear a child crying — the sound seemed to be coming from inside the doors. Slowly, she moved closer to the entrance.

She could barely make out the stairs that

descended into the black dungeon below. The weeping had changed to a whimper and then softened altogether until she could hear nothing. Ashley thought about calling down into the darkness, but something made her keep her silence.

Soon she heard movement from deep within the cavern. Someone, it seemed, was dragging something across the floor toward the entrance of the cellar. The hair on the back of Ashley's neck stood on end as she listened. She longed to run, but she knew there was no escape. That was when she began to feel the pulling sensation. At first, it felt like a gentle nudge, as though someone was inside her begging for room. Against a painful, physical yanking she fought for what felt like an eternity. Suddenly the scuffing sound ceased, but Ashley couldn't see beyond the shadows in the fruit cellar. And then, the pulling sensation stopped. All she could hear was the sound of her own breathing.

A moment later, it stepped into the light. Ashley recoiled with revulsion. A scream rose in her throat, but refused to come out. There in the moonlight, at the base of the stairs, was a child who looked not much older than fourteen. The woman-child was dressed in a cotton nightgown that touched the floor. Her long hair was loose around her shoulders as though she had risen from sleep. From her waist down, the white gown she wore was soaked with water and blood.

She reached out, said, "Momma," then collapsed.

Ashley woke in a sweat, half-crazed from the

nightmare. She flung off the sheets and ran out of the room. Since the nightmares started getting so bad, she had made it a habit to leave the kitchen light on. It was the one place she felt safe from the intrusion.

Almost instantly, the phone rang. Ashley stared at it. At length, she came back to herself and answered it.

It was Emily, who was almost frantic. "Babe, are you all right?"

Ashley had to swallow two or three times before she could respond. Her mouth felt dry. "Yeah," she said thickly.

"My God, I just got the most vivid psychic impression from you. I thought you were dead."

"No. I'm fine."

"What happened? One of your nightmares again?"

"Yeah."

Emily softened her voice. "What happened?"

Ashley began to cry as she recounted the dream to Emily. At the end she added, "The child. The child in the dream was me."

"You mean she looked like you," Emily corrected.

"No," Ashley said, swallowing her tears. "I mean that it was me."

Ashley couldn't fall back to sleep for the remainder of the night. She waited, with the help of a pot of coffee, for the still rays of the morning sun to hit the sliding glass doors of her apartment. By that time, she had showered and dressed.

She climbed into her car and drove to her mother's house with the hopes of speaking to her about the disturbing dream. She was greeted at the door by her mother's live-in housekeeper and cook. She told Ashley that Patricia was occupied in the study and would probably be out soon. Ashley found a lounge chair on the rear balcony and sat down. She hoped that it wouldn't be a long wait, though she knew her mother and what she was doing in the study.

Patricia had been making her solitary, early-morning retreats into the study from the time Ashley's father died. Ashley privately wondered if Patricia really could speak to him and why. Their marriage had been hard and filled with pain.

Ashley's father drank himself to death. He died the year that Ashley graduated from high school. It was the worst time of her life. Despite everything, she loved her father with all his faults and missed him to this day.

On the other side of the house, Patricia was engaged in a conversation with Marshal, her late husband.

Patricia always met him on the plane between this life and the next — it would be too dangerous to cross over completely. They always met in the same place, a sacred place, to Patricia, that recalled her early childhood. She thought it was the safest place on either side.

Patricia sat comfortably on a flat rock that

overlooked a small babbling creek that flowed like a ribbon through the forest. She was smiling. Marshal sat next to her and held her hand.

The two had been silent for a long time before Patricia said, "I'm worried about Ashley. She's been having those awful dreams. But Emily told me she thought that something was trying to possess Ashley."

Marshal looked concerned but kept quiet.

Irritated, Patricia asked, "What do you think?"

Marshal raised his hand as if preparing to ward off a physical attack. "You know that I can't tell you that. Listen, tell Ashley to be careful where she goes. There's an evil pursuing her." With that Marshal began to fade.

Patricia wondered at his words that sent a chill down her back. She knew in her heart the words he had spoken were true. The question was, how would she tell Ashley?

"I am telling you what your father told me this morning," Patricia said, angry. With her usual flare she had boldly announced Marshal's presentiment. Not for a moment did she think Ashley would doubt her.

Ashley rested her forehead on her hands. "I can't believe you sometimes, Mother. You really expect me to believe that some evil has been chasing the women on your side of the family for generations? And this other thing about Poppa. Sometimes I think Becky's right."

"Right about what?"

"Never mind, Mother."

"Ashley, I won't accept this talking behind my back. What did Becky say?"

"She said that sometimes she thinks that you never got over Poppa's death. She said that's why you invent these outrageous stories about meeting him somewhere between both worlds." Ashley stopped and bit her lip.

Patricia was hurt. "So both my daughters think I'm crazy, huh," she said. "I may be eccentric in my own way, Ashley, but I am far from being crazy. I resent my children snickering behind my back like old Mrs. Palmaroy's sons did all those years. The poor woman."

Ashley rose. "Look, Mother, Mrs. Palmaroy was nuts, but that's not the point. I appreciate what you're saying, but I think that you read too many of those damned books that come through the store. That and that overactive imagination of yours create things that are simply not true."

Patricia, still angered by her daughter's doubts, shook her finger. "Someday you'll know there are things out there that should not be taken lightly. I have never lied to any of my children. I know what I know because I have an open mind, because I know that the gift I have is real. And you can bury your head in the sand and pretend you don't know things before they happen, that you can't see people's thoughts or the past events of some people's lives running through your mind like a movie, but I will not. You can only fight the truth for so long before it bites you right on the butt."

Ashley sighed. "I didn't come here to fight with you, Mother. I only wanted to tell you about the dreams and to try to sort out what it means, and I didn't feel like going to Emily's. The stuff about Poppa upsets me." Noticeably, she relaxed and went on. "I'll take your words to heart, Mother. I'm sorry if I insinuated you're crazy. You're not. Just sometimes I don't know what to do with some of the things you say." Ashley leaned over and gave her mother a hug.

Patricia gave in. She suspected there was more truth to Marshal's words than she cared to admit. She feared that Ashley was walking a dangerous line. If Marshal was right, Ashley would need her help. She decided to take his advice and accept Emily's invitation to the bed-and-breakfast, especially now that Ashley had decided to go. She shivered with the thought that it might be her daughter's only salvation.

CHAPTER SIX

Ashley could feel her stomach turn to jelly when she saw Catherine standing on the large front porch of the old house. The Pacific breeze lifted her black, wavy hair from her shoulders as though admiring it. Catherine shaded her eyes and surveyed the view. Ashley found herself mesmerized by the curves of Catherine's body, the slim waist, the long, tanned, well-muscled legs.

"Come on, Ash," Emily said, poking her in the ribs with a long fingernail. Ashley tore herself away and shut off the car. It was a perfect fall day and she decided not to put up the top of the convertible right away. Maybe she'd sneak out later and take a drive along the coastline.

"Hey, Catherine," Emily called as she stepped out of the car. She wore a brightly colored, long flowing skirt and equally vivid top. Catherine waved from the porch.

"Sure as hell doesn't look like much," Ashley said, walking up alongside Emily with their luggage.

The entire house stood stoically overlooking the ocean. The whitewash on the old mansion had peeled off long ago and the lawn that once dominated at least an acre of the huge estate had gone to ragweed. Wild rosebushes ran rampant along the ocean, but everything was still green and the air smelled fresh.

"Where is everybody?" Emily asked as she made her way up to the porch.

Catherine shrugged as she watched Ashley bring up the luggage. "I thought you said they were revamping the place to convert it into a bed-and-breakfast," she said, shoving her hands into her pockets.

Emily tried the heavy door, but found it locked. She wiped her hand across the window and felt a slight vibration run through her body. "Catherine," she said without turning from the window. "Come here and see, would you? Put your hand against the glass." As quickly as she put it there, she pulled her hand away. Her eyes grew dark.

Emily understood what she was thinking. In her years as a medium, she had only felt a vibration like that once — in the wake of a witch when she passed by. Totally black aura. Emily shuddered. Perhaps this mission was not going to be as simple as she thought. She thanked herself for bringing all the various tools of her trade. She'd probably need them all before the weekend was said and done.

"Hello, Ashley," Catherine said, her voice and eyes softening.

Ashley nodded.

"Where's Patricia?"

Ashley squinted. "I imagine she'll be around shortly."

"Madame Mistorie?" a voice inquired.

Emily felt her soul leap two stories high. Everyone turned to find an elderly couple standing before them on the porch. Emily smiled quickly to hide her fear.

"Yes," she said, holding out her hand to the gray-haired man. "Mr. Dupree, I presume."

He shook her hand with a firm and sure grip. "Yes. Sorry we're so late, but the wife couldn't find the key." He nodded toward the woman who smiled but said nothing. She was a small, timid thing with a look of total submission on her face. Emily caught a look in the woman's eyes that seemed almost afraid. She dismissed it for the moment as the group filed into the house. Patricia joined them as they stood in the foyer.

Emily gasped with amazement at the interior of the house that had falsely looked so ruined from the outside. The interior was painstakingly restored to its original decor, an obvious fashion statement in its time.

"There are fifteen bedrooms upstairs," Mr. Dupree

was saying, "not counting the maid's quarters. A huge, what we would call industrial-size kitchen downstairs. A complete study, a small ballroom, a sitting room, several family rooms depending on your mood, a formal dining room, and a greenhouse added onto the back by the last people who lived here. The history of the house is a bit lost in obscurity, but I can assure you ladies that it is haunted by a good many ghosts and some are not the friendly type."

He continued before even Emily could get a word in, "I assume that all of you will be staying here for the duration of the investigation, or exorcism, or whatever it is, so I took the liberty of having some of the bedrooms done up for you. I also got a gal from town to come up and stay with you while you're here. She'll be taking care of the cooking and other needs so that you can concentrate on our otherworld friends."

Emily finally found her opening. "I need to know what you and the others have been seeing, hearing and feeling in the house and on the grounds. If you could make a list with as much detail as possible, it would really help us."

Dupree nodded as he pulled a white handkerchief out of his back pocket and wiped his face. A portly man, dressed in a gray suit and red tie, he was perspiring heavily as the group made its way to the second floor. He stopped several times as they went and each time he had something to say. "The third level is not refinished yet and I would advise that you not do much poking around up there. It's nothing to look at right now anyway," he cautioned, his face flushed. Emily nodded, wishing they could move at a faster pace. She was looking forward to seeing Teri.

Later that afternoon, Ashley had the strange feeling that she had somehow been at the house before, but it escaped her when she tried to think about it. She decided to unpack her suitcase and enjoy the large, beautifully decorated bedroom.

Emily had taken the room adjoining Ashley's and Catherine took the room adjacent to Patricia's across the hall.

It wasn't long before Ashley heard her mother bumping up the stairs and down the hall. Thinking she'd help Patricia unpack, she turned from her window, where she had been enjoying the view of the ocean, and nearly ran straight into a young woman standing before her.

The woman was clad in a dress made of what looked like silk. Her face was bunched with worry and she ran her rosary beads between her fingers nervously. She seemed to be crying. For a moment, all Ashley could do was stare at her — she seemed so clearly out of place.

When she asked, "Who are you?" the woman vanished. Ashley's heart thumped against her chest so hard she was afraid she might be having a coronary. All she could do was breathe slowly and tell herself it was merely a trick her mind was playing on her. But trick or not, she decided to find someone else to be with at the moment.

She found Emily being entertained in the kitchen

by a handsome woman with a slightly overweight build that looked good on her. She wore her hair shoulder-length and parted to one side. Dressed in cut-offs and a tank top that exposed her deep tan, she smiled easily, her gaze reflecting an interest in one of Emily's tall tales of the supernatural.

Ashley cleared her throat as she walked into the immense kitchen. Emily shot her a look as if to say, "If she asks you anything, just go along with it."

"Teri, this is my very best friend Ashley. Teri works for Mr. Dupree sometimes and will be cooking for us."

Ashley could tell from the quick introduction that Emily wanted her to take the clue and leave them alone.

"How do you do," Ashley said, shaking Teri's hand.

"Nice to meet you," Teri said, exposing the dimples on her cheeks.

Emily butted in, "Patricia got her luggage. Did you see her?"

Ashley nodded.

"I think she wanted to talk to you." Emily's eyes were pleading with Ashley to go elsewhere.

"Ah, my mother. Yes, I think that would be a good idea. Incidentally, where's Catherine?" Emily shrugged and turned her attention back to the handsome woman who had caught her eye.

Ashley was about to go stir-crazy in the strangely quiet house and wandered outside to explore the grounds. For what she wasn't sure. She came around the side of the house and saw Catherine standing near a great rosebed. Ashley could smell their sweet scent. The only thing sweeter was the look on

Catherine's face as she stood there in a daydream. Ashley wondered what she was thinking, if she should approach her at all.

She was still contemplating leaving when Catherine turned to her. The time for flight had passed and she had to say something, anything. "Hi," she managed shyly. Catherine smiled. Ashley came a little closer half-expecting Catherine to explode with accusations at any moment. Rather, she stood there silently, twirling a blade of grass in her fingers.

Ashley finally broke the silence. "Listen, I'm sorry about what happened. I, well, I didn't know, you know, that you were straight."

Catherine smiled softly. "In fact, I'm engaged, but would it have mattered?"

Ashley gulped. "Probably not." It had been hard enough to accept that Catherine was straight, but engaged?

Catherine laughed softly as if reading her thoughts.

"I told him I didn't want a ring." Ashley relaxed.

For a long while the two women walked around the grounds. Apparently, the engagement was more or less arranged by Catherine's mother.

"So what made you decide to take a sabbatical up here away from your fiancé. If the wedding's three weeks away, shouldn't you be frantically trying to pull together last-minute details? Even a small wedding's a lot of work..."

Catherine shrugged. "I should think that it would be obvious."

Ashley wondered at that for a time before she decided to play stupid. "What do you mean?"

Catherine stopped and turned to meet Ashley's

gaze. "You've forced me think about who I am. It infuriated my mother, but she's not living my life." Ashley still wasn't sure what she meant, but she nodded sympathetically and inwardly rejoiced at the possibilities that may lie ahead for her and Catherine.

That night, after the meeting with Mr. Dupree where he had recited his list of strange occurrences, Ashley thought about Catherine until she fell into a deep sleep. The first part of the night she did not dream at all, but the second part of the night was filled with haunting images.

There was a child playing on the earthen floor in a musty-smelling room with no windows. The child looked enough like Ashley to be her own. She was singing a nonsensical little song and fiddling with a tiny rag doll with hair made out of shreds of yellow fabric.

The room was lit only with a kerosene lamp that burned dully on a ledge carved out of the wall. Ashley could barely make out the stairs behind her. She knew by instinct that the double doors were closed and locked from the outside. Her gaze turned to the short narrow hallway in which the child played. The floor was cool as she moved closer to the end of the hallway. The child smiled briefly, her face paled by lack of sunlight. Ashley wondered if she was alone inside this dungeon.

At the end of the hallway, she encountered two separate byways. In the light of the kerosene lamp, she saw a makeshift bed piled with quilts. On top of the bed lay the same woman she had seen in another dream. She seemed older, yet she still looked like Ashley. In the other room, she found a slop bucket and a wash basin with water in it. A chill ran the length of her spine.

The child suddenly appeared. "Momma," she said, pulling on the woman's skirts. The woman stirred and looked down into the deep blue eyes. "I'm hungry."

The woman smiled reassuringly. "I know, baby, but we need to wait until Grandfather leaves so that Rinee can bring us our morning meal." The child seemed satisfied with that and returned to her doll.

Ashley watched, a silent witness, as the woman slumped back on the bed. She foraged around until she found what she had been seeking among the many heaps of quilts. It was a sort of diary that reminded Ashley of a modern-day ledger, only thicker. When she found the inkwell and pen, the woman began to scrawl inside the book. It was not until Ashley saw the date, that she realized she was back inside the same dream that had been coming to her in bits and pieces.

She read what the woman wrote, though she felt that the words there were personal, intended for no one else. It felt almost like she was forced to read the words, for the harder she resisted, the more she felt drawn to look. The handwriting was simple and childlike. She misspelled words and used simple phrases.

Momma seys it has ben four years sense I have ben down in the celer. My child Elowese has lived here for that long to. I wish I could see my sister Margaret again so I can talk to her. I wish I new why God wants to punish me so. I must be evil becase that is wut Poppa ust to tell me and he sed the devil wold cum and take away childrn who ly. So wen Momma ask I sed no thing. And then she brung me here. I had a babee then to. I dont think Poppa know abowt that otherwize he wold sent the devil to take her away. We must be very quiet when he is home cuz he think I ded. Sometimes I wish I was.

It was signed *Rebecca Winslow, 1896*

Catherine woke to the sound of church bells ringing in the distance. She threw a robe on, and went to the window. At first she couldn't find the source of the pealing bells, and then, as she leaned out her window, she saw off to the far right a large building made of roughly hewn stone. It seemed to be an old convent, unlike any she had ever seen. After a pause, the bells chimed exactly six times before a still silence filled the morning air. She knew that the bells were summoning the sisters for the morning prayers.

Suddenly, the convent dissipated almost as if it had been a mirage or an illusion. Had it been an illusion? But when she looked again, only rubble and the two crumbing walls remained. She decided there was certainly more to this place than anyone thought. She shivered and pulled her robe closer, for an abrupt chill filled the room.

As she turned from the window she found the reason for the sudden temperature drop. There stood before her two women, one with fair skin and the other with dark brown skin. She could almost see through them. They seemed oblivious to Catherine's presence — or if they knew she was there they chose to ignore her. Catherine sensed a drama about to unfold.

The fair-skinned woman, who appeared to be no older than seventeen, was dressed in a fine gown of yellow silk, with tiny bows circling the base of the skirt. The other looked a few years older and wore a sturdy dress of cotton. Catherine could see where it had been mended many times in the past. It was made for comfort and ease in care.

There were tears in the eyes of both of the women as they embraced. It was a tender embrace reserved for lovers. When their lips met, Catherine stared.

The dark-skinned woman was the first to pull away. Through her tears she asked, "Why won't you leave with me today?"

The other woman absent-mindedly picked up a pearl-handled hairbrush. "Where would we go? Who would take in the likes of us? I must go. Poppa is furious and jealous of my friendship with you. He thinks that the devil has possessed you, and you have led me from the right path."

"Jesus is my savior. I know nothing of the devil, but I know that I love you."

"God preserve us all through this," the pale-skinned woman said, touching the black bruises on her face.

"The things he has done to you all these years, and yet you would follow your father off the cliffs if he so beckoned you," the other woman said, her dark face pinched in pain.

49

"Margaret, come. Now," a man hollered from beyond the closed door.

Margaret shivered and her eyes mirrored the dark-skinned woman's pain. Once more they embraced.

"Write me and leave your notes in the convent wall. I will find them and write you back," Margaret said as she shut the door behind her.

When she was certain her lover was gone, the dark-skinned woman knelt to the floor and wept. Through her tears, she uttered a single prayer as they faded from the room.

For a long moment, Catherine stared at the place where the woman had knelt. Her mind raced. She had no words for what she saw, but she knew the true feeling that sprang from the drama that played out before her: anguish.

CHAPTER SEVEN

Emily was all smiles at the morning breakfast. Catherine was quiet. Patricia droned on and on about the first thing she thought they should do. Apparently she was the only one who had heard a thing Mr. Dupree had said the evening before. Ashley sat back in her own quietness and thought about the latest dream that haunted her.

Over the melon salad Teri served, Emily said, "First, has anyone had any psychic impressions or seen or felt anything out of the ordinary since we've been here?"

Patricia spoke first. "Nope. I slept like a baby last night."

Emily nodded. "So did I."

I'll bet, Ashley thought, smiling.

"Ashley or Catherine, anything to report?" Emily asked.

"Well, Sergeant," Ashley teased.

"Cut it with that," Emily replied playfully.

"Sorry, just playing around. Listen, I had another dream last night about the girl in the cellar. It was really bizarre. She kept a journal of some sort and she was writing about her father and her sister named Margaret." Ashley realized she was squeezing her napkin in her hand.

"I don't know if it really has anything to do with this, though," Emily said skeptically.

Catherine interrupted, "I think that it just might."

This pulled Patricia to inquire, "How so?"

Catherine mentioned the experience she had had earlier that morning and finished with, "The woman's name was Margaret."

Everyone remained quiet for a long moment.

Finally Emily conceded, "You know, I just wonder if the two situations aren't related in some way."

"I think we had better approach this thing very carefully," Patricia said.

For the first time in a long time, Ashley saw the fear in her mother's eyes. Patricia was serious. Ashley nodded in agreement. "I don't think we really knew what we were dealing with when we first decided to come here. Hell, I thought that it would be a vacation. But maybe I was wrong."

A sudden chill filled the room and the air became as dense as a fog shroud. No one moved. Something was coming from beyond. Something that had the power of darkness on its side. Ashley felt the old familiar pulling that had become commonplace in her dreams. She fought the invisible hands that grasped her. The strength had ebbed out of her. She could not win.

"Oh, my God," Patricia said, her eyes wide with shock. Above her daughter, who sat in a death-like trance, two wispy figures were locked in mortal combat. They seemed to spin around each other, sometimes becoming as one in the confusion. Neither face was distinct, but clearly these were shadows of former selves fighting for possession of Ashley's body. Patricia was scared.

Catherine dug into the pockets of her jeans and pulled out a small pouch. "It's my mother's rosary," she explained hastily. "Blessed by Pope John Paul." She rose from the table and placed the rosary around Ashley's neck.

Almost instantly a single voice cried out in agony. Ashley opened her eyes and grabbed for the beads as she cried, "It burns, take it off, it burns." Catherine remained steadfast as Patricia gasped, utterly immobilized, helpless in her fear.

Slowly, Ashley began to gain some ground against the enemy as she came back to herself. Profuse beads of sweat ran down her face and her eyes reflected the terror inside her.

Finally, the apparition seemed to let go. Ashley's body sagged as a kind of fury seemed to envelope the room. Patricia felt its evilness.

"You have not won, whore," it declared as it vanished. "There will be another time when you shall once again be my possession. And I will live."

At first, Ashley wasn't sure where she was. The faces that surrounded her were filled with fear and apprehension. After a moment, she recognized the dining room in the old house and muttered, "What is it? What happened?"

Emily tried to smile off her worries. "You wouldn't believe it if I told you."

Ashley nodded. "You're probably right, but try me."

Patricia wrapped her arm around her daughter protectively. "We're not sure what happened. Are you all right?"

Ashley thought for a moment, trying to clear the fog in her brain. She remembered the room growing colder and the prickling of her skin. And then the pulling. The rest was a blur.

Emily inserted, "Like hell we don't know what happened. It was the worst case of possession I have ever witnessed. Catherine here saved you."

"I don't believe you. You and your overactive imagination. That was all it was." Emily looked hurt and Ashley wished that she could take back her words. She was frightened. Something had happened, she just wasn't sure what.

"Look, Ashley, do you think that I made this up too." Emily parted Ashley's shirt. Ashley got up and looked in the mirror over the sideboard. There were burns on her neck. "Whatever it was, it was real."

"And pissed," Patricia added seriously.

Catherine said, "I've seen things like this all over the world. Some are considered demonic possessions."

Ashley laughed aloud and started to leave.

Catherine put a hand on her shoulder. "I've seen things that would make a true believer out of anyone in this room." Her eyes changed a shade darker and Ashley knew she was telling the truth. "In Haiti, where I served the church for a few years, I saw women and men become possessed by spirits of their long-dead relatives. It is a ritual. A custom. Through certain rites and procedures, the priestess invites the spirits into herself and completely relinquishes control of her body. It is considered a great honor for them."

Ashley frowned. "So what you're saying is that one of my long-dead relatives wants to possess me and I'm supposed to let them."

Catherine looked into her eyes. "No. I'm saying it's a possibility. From what I saw, there was more than one spirit fighting to possess your body. At first I thought that it was your soul until I noticed one thing." Catherine's gaze rested on each of them in turn. "She wore a gold crucifix."

"This is what I think we should do. First of all, I don't think that any of us should be alone in this house or on the grounds. It's entirely too dangerous, especially after what just happened to Ashley," Emily said, pacing the floor.

The women had gathered an hour after the attack on Ashley to decide what should be done to protect themselves from any further attacks. Teri was invited in on the conversation since Emily felt that it concerned her as well.

"I think we're just a bit too jumpy here. I don't think that I need someone to hold my hand all the time," Ashley said cynically.

Emily stopped in midstride. "Ashley, dear, you may not remember that attack on you, but the rest of us do. I think it would be safer for all of us if we didn't underestimate what's going on here."

"What's going on here? I think our imaginations are all in high gear, and if we're not careful, we'll all end up shooting our own feet off. I don't think that the psychic power is so great in this house. It's just our collective fears," Ashley said, trying to explain away some of the tension she felt in the room.

Emily sighed. "Ashley, if it hadn't been for Catherine, God only knows what would have happened to you in there. And I, for one, am not willing to find out. Please, just hear us out."

Ashley shrugged. "Fine." Even though Emily sometimes took herself way too seriously, deep in Ashley's heart, she knew that something happened over breakfast and that the residue it had left behind made her shudder inside.

"Now, this is what we know. One, that Ashley's dreams and this place may very well be one and the same, which means that there's probably a fruit cellar around here someplace. Teri, any ideas?"

Teri shrugged, "I don't know. As a kid I never came up here because people in town said it was haunted by evil spirits. Supposedly people came up here to perform blood sacrifices and things like that."

"Great," Patricia said, rubbing the goosebumps on her arms. "This house is not only haunted, it's the home for devil-worshiping sacrifices to boot."

Teri grinned reassuringly. "Now, Patricia, those were just rumors. I think that most of that was meant to keep me away from a rotting old house."

Patricia smiled, but clearly she was not reassured. In fact, Ashley guessed she was more frightened now than ever.

"I think that we should spread out into groups and search the house and the grounds for any psychic impressions. Or any physical things that might help us understand this. It's obvious we're dealing with more than one spirit here, and with something other than the most gracious of hosts. I think the key to setting them to rest lies with unraveling what happened here." Emily paused for any comments or reactions.

There were nods of general agreement.

"Then I say that Catherine and Ashley go and explore the house from top to bottom. And I mean the third floor as well. Patricia, Teri and I will scour the grounds and see if we can find that fruit cellar."

Catherine and Ashley soon found that accessing the third floor would be a lot rougher than they thought. Someone, quite recently in fact, had taken pains to install a heavy oak door and a clasp lock, effectively blocking off the third-floor stairway. The thing that puzzled Catherine was that the lock looked fairly new.

The two women spent almost thirty minutes prying open the clasp. They discovered that the screws that held the clasp were a good two inches long, and there were four of them.

Catherine said, "It looks like someone was trying to keep someone out."

Ashley nodded with a grin. "Or something in."

At last the door swung open on squeaky hinges. The pungent odor of age and decay assaulted them. This was part of the house no one had bothered to remodel yet, and it looked as though no one had stirred here in a long time.

"After you, Madame," Ashley said, holding the door open for Catherine.

Catherine shook her head. "Oh, no, after you. I insist."

Ashley stepped into the frame of the door and paused, as if she wasn't sure what she was looking or listening for, but just as Ashley moved to climb the stairs, Catherine heard something. It wasn't a loud sound, more like a rustling.

Ashley turned to her. "Did you hear that?"

Catherine frowned. "Kinda, what was it? Mice?"

"Maybe. Or a curtain. Probably a window open somewhere. Drafts." She smiled.

"Sure," Catherine said smiling uneasily. She nudged Ashley up the stairs.

Catherine felt a tiny flutter in her stomach as she remembered the night that Ashley had kissed her on the beach. It was a memory that replayed itself often in her mind whether she wanted it to or not. There was no question what the feeling was that rose with the memory. But it couldn't be that, she told herself as she watched Ashley ascend the stairs ahead of her. It was her own doubts, her own fears, and the discovery that she may not be the woman she thought she was. It was strange. She was always self-assured and secure in what she thought she wanted and needed. Now this. Certainly, if she could believe her own heart, things would never be the way they were before.

At the top of the stairs, the hallway split in two directions. At one time, Catherine reasoned, this had probably been the servants' quarters. Ashley went searching for the back entrance the servants would have used to access their rooms from the kitchen rather than the main stairs.

Catherine noticed a waist-high pedestal with an oil lamp on it. Next to it was a handful of matches. The oil lamp seemed out of place and it took her a moment before she knew why. "Look at this, Ashley," Catherine called over her shoulder.

"It's an oil lamp, Catherine," Ashley said sarcastically.

"But look at this." Catherine ran her finger along the beveled glass top. There was no dust. Everything else, including the pedestal, had a heavy layer of dust on it.

Ashley shrugged. "Probably somebody used it before the electricity was installed." She touched the lamp and quickly drew back her hand. She shook her head. "Strange. There's a humming in my ear. It's far away. It's . . . a child crying."

* * * * *

Patricia stepped lightly through the waist-high weeds that littered the once-extravagant grounds that belonged to the huge mansion. Rosebeds, interspersed with perennial borders, dotted the grounds, but all were nearly choked out by the ragweed. The remains of a swing hung from one huge oak that loomed over what once must have been a green and plush carpet of lawn. There was still a gazebo built from rocks.

Patricia closed her eyes for a moment and tried to imagine what it was like back then. The beautiful women in their elegant gowns, the handsome men in their trousers, the gleeful children in their Sunday best. She could almost smell the exquisite food coming from the big house. People were laughing, engaged in slow conversations under parasols or in the gazebo. She opened her mind further and imagined she was a part of the splendor.

Patricia felt the firm touch of a large hand on her elbow and she opened her eyes, squinting in the full sunlight.

"Judith," a man she did not recognize said, a touch of the South in his accent.

Patricia was startled beyond her own elaborate imagination. The man stood a good foot taller than her. His hair was white and his beard full but neatly trimmed. His eyes reflected a coldness that she had never seen in a man before.

"Judith," the man said firmly, his grip on her elbow so tight Patricia feared she would be bruised. "Have you gone daft?" he demanded. His brows were furrowed.

All she could do was nod. Around her, the images she had created in her mind became reality, or she thought, shivering, she had clearly become a part of theirs.

Dressed in a wide array of spring colors, Patricia was stunned by the beauty of their costumes. Women stood under parasols. She glanced at her own reflection on the water in the pond she stood next to. She looked much older. Her face was pinched with the lines of worry and age beyond her own years. Her body felt frail. She took in the dress she wore. The white collar of the costume was stiff and came to the top of her neck.

Her soft, blue silk shirt puffed out into full Bishop sleeves and narrowed at her wrists. A full skirt made of fine wool serge fell from her small waist and hid her feet. She wore pearl colored, four-button kid gloves. A frilly parasol shaded her from the sun.

When she looked up, the man still stood beside her.

"What *is* it," Patricia asked, trying to swallow the dryness that had formed in her throat.

The man's face remained stern. "What is it? Is that the way to address your husband? I have asked you several times to get Margaret and bring her down here. This is her party, after all, and I don't want any excuses this time, or there will be hell to pay for both of you. Understand me?"

Patricia nodded, fear building in her gut. She squeezed her eyes tight and closed her mind against the images. She refused to open her eyes until the pounding of her heart returned to normal and she could no longer feel the hand on her elbow.

Slowly, Patricia opened her eyes. The grounds

were a disarray of weeds and flowers. She sighed heavily. That was close, she thought as she picked her way through the immense yard. Somewhere in the back of her mind, a memory stirred like a butterfly and elusively fluttered away when she reached for it.

Emily paused for a moment as she and Teri slowly combed the area. "I thought I felt something, but it passed by me so quickly I'm not sure." She shrugged.

Teri looked at her doubtfully. She thought for the most part that Emily was putting her on. Still, she loved to hear Emily's stories. It had been so long since she had met someone like Emily.

She tried to remember the last time that she was in Portland and had met anyone who wasn't straight. She couldn't recall. Teri had responsibilities other than herself and her needs. She had a daughter that she had not told Emily about yet.

Her daughter, Gretchen, had disappeared almost three months ago, and every day of her life since then was devoted to finding her. She had very little time to think about anything else, let alone pursue a social life. Until last night. For once she had relaxed her guard and let someone in. She trusted Emily because of who she was.

Emily touched her arm. "Are you all right?"

Teri nodded and gave a faint smile. She had wanted to wait to tell Emily about Gretchen, but this was as good a time as any. Besides, she didn't want to get deeply involved with someone who couldn't accept her life as a whole.

"Listen, Emily, I have something to tell you. It's really hard for me so please, don't say anything until I'm finished."

"Go on," Emily said. There was a look of unconcealed concern on her face.

"I have a daughter who will be ten this year. She, she . . . She disappeared two months, three weeks, and four days ago. I was doing some renovations up here, working for the owners, when she just disappeared. I haven't heard from her since. For a long time, I worried that she fell over the cliff, but she was a smart child. She knew better than to play there, and of course, we thought about the forest behind the house, but the search parties couldn't find a trace of her. She —" Teri paused to wipe the tears away from her eyes. "She just disappeared. She was all I had and she's just gone."

Emily pulled Teri close to her and wrapped her arms tightly around her. For a long time she held her, and Teri let herself cry. Emily stroked her hair and talked softly to her. Gradually, Teri calmed down.

"This is what I need you to do," Emily said, lifting Teri's chin. Teri looked at her. "Get something very personal that belonged to your daughter, that she loved very much, and bring it back here. You may not believe in the powers that the three of us possess, but you will."

CHAPTER EIGHT

In a circle around the dining room table, the women shared their experiences and what they had found. Patricia shared her story first and the others stared in astonishment. It was becoming clear that the house held something terribly disturbing.

Ashley shivered with the thought that passed through her mind. "Mother, did you say the woman was named Judith?"

"That was what he called me. 'Judith, have you gone daft,' is what he said."

Ashley nodded. "In my dreams the woman is called Judith. I don't know how I know this, I just do. Like a given, but never said. And that man, he sounds like the one in the dreams. I can see his face clearly in my mind. My God, am I dreaming about a real place and real people?"

Catherine said, "It's entirely possible, but why would you have dreams about a place before seeing it? What I mean is, it's not unusual to capture psychic images from the impressions left in houses, especially one this old, but why would you be dreaming about it before coming here?"

Ashley grinned, "I thought *I* was the Holy Doubter." She added seriously, "I've been having these dreams for years and so has Patricia, and Grandma too." Her gaze went to Patricia who was pressing a brightly painted fingernail to her lips. She offered no information.

Everyone turned to Emily when she said, "Pat, have you ever dreamed of these people before or had any images like this in the past?"

Patricia shook her head. "My dreams were never as vivid as Ashley's. I mean, I dreamed about a great house overlooking an ocean, and I remember a woman in my dreams, but I never knew her name. I've never seen that man before today, dreams or otherwise."

"This is all very odd," Emily said, crossing her legs underneath her long full black skirt.

Catherine shrugged. "Could it be that the past somehow has enough power in this instance to somehow manifest itself to someone who is strong enough psychically to pick it up?"

Patricia disagreed. "That's possible only when the person is present where the actual people lived, breathed, loved and died."

They all shook their heads glumly. The closer they got to the truth the farther away it seemed to run.

Emily changed the subject. "There's something I'm going to need your help on. It seems that Teri has a daughter." She held up her hand to ward off the questions enthusiastically aimed at her. "Let me finish. She disappeared almost three months ago from here and Teri believes she may still be alive somewhere." Emily's shoulders slumped a bit. "I don't see how. She was only ten years old when she disappeared. With all things considered." Her voice faded off.

Ashley could feel the mood of the room go from bleak to downright gloomy.

"If Emily is thinking what I'm thinking," Catherine said, "there may be a way for us to let Teri know one way or the other. And Pat, you should know the uncanny ability of a mother to know things about the safety of her child. Maybe Teri knows inside her heart that she's safe."

"Teri does know," a voice said softly from the entranceway to the dining room.

Everyone turned. Teri was holding a small worn teddy bear tightly in her hands. Her face was a study of tension and grief. For the first time, Ashley could see the real person behind the façade of smiles and high spirits. It seemed that Teri had almost reached her end, when dying or putting it to a final rest were the only options.

Emily put her arm tenderly around Teri and led her to the table. Catherine stood and pulled out a chair for her. Emily kissed the woman on the brow before she announced, "This is what I have in mind." Quickly, she explained what she wanted done and how it could be accomplished. Everyone agreed that it sounded like a positive plan. They decided to meet in the cozy room that once served as a parlor.

An hour later, everyone gathered in the parlor. The sun had set, and Patricia was turning on the low lamps strategically placed around the room. Teri looked like she had enough time to compose herself, for she was smiling cheerfully. The teddy bear was sitting on one of the heavy old end tables that had been pulled out into the center of the room.

Patricia, Catherine, Emily and Teri were seated around it on the floor by the time that Ashley came in. She was disappointed to find that Catherine was already flanked by her mother and Emily. She took her place next to Teri.

"This was Gretchen's favorite teddy bear. She's had the darned thing since she was a baby. My mother bought it for her. It's the one thing I know she loved more than anything in the whole world," Teri said softly, holding the bear and looking at each of them. She handed the stuffed toy to Emily who gently touched it as though she were stroking a child.

Her eyes closed, and Ashley knew she was clearing her mind. She would still all thoughts that flooded her whenever she tried to concentrate this way. She would coach herself to assure that nothing remained in her head except for a deep silence and darkness.

Emily could feel her muscles relax as she focused on the silence that filled her mind. Carefully, she allowed one thought to enter. She called for the child named Gretchen. Over and over she let the name pass through the stillness. Over and over she called.

From deep within her, she could hear a voice. It was a tiny, frightened voice that called into the night. It was the voice of a child. Emily called for her in her mind. The child responded with words that Emily could not hear clearly enough to understand. She called again and the voice became clearer.

"Mommy?" Over and over again, the child repeated the word as though pleading with the darkness to open and let her out.

Soon, the voice faded to stillness. Emily couldn't get the child to answer her question, but one thing was certain, she was alive. She could feel it in her gut.

Emily opened her eyes and allowed the clouds of the trance to wear off before she said, "Gretchen is still alive. There's no question about that." She didn't volunteer anymore information. She didn't want to taint the findings of the other women.

Teri breathed a long sigh of relief. "I knew it, I knew she was still alive. I would know if something had happened to her. We're close. I would know."

Emily reasoned that Teri's conviction had allowed her to hold on this long without going insane.

Patricia took the bear and placed the toy close to her heart. She emptied her mind quickly and concentrated on the child. It didn't take her long to pick up on her whereabouts.

The place was dark, very dark. She sensed that wherever it was, there were no windows and only a single door. She felt as though the child was in the middle of a small, cramped room. She couldn't stand fully and she could only move in a small radius.

Patricia gasped as she realized that the child had some sort of a chain around her ankle, like a shackle. Sometimes the metal caused her pain — when it was fastened too tight or chafed from too much movement. The chain was long enough for her to reach a makeshift potty on the other side of the room. Thankfully, fresh air came in from somewhere overhead so that the child didn't suffocate.

Patricia sensed that the child had long since given up on trying to find a way out, that she had begun to believe the things she'd been told, that she'd given up on her mother ever finding her.

At the moment, the child seemed to be sleeping. Her breathing was shallow, as if she was dreaming. Patricia couldn't tap into the dream, but she knew that the dream was frightening to her.

Slowly, her mind began to withdraw. "She's alive. I can still feel her consciousness. It feels ..." Patricia paused to clarify her thoughts. "It feels like she's close, very close."

* * * * *

Ashley saw her mother's face pinch with concern and concentration. She took the bear and was instantly accosted with images of the past.

In her mind, Ashley saw the child wandering around the grounds that had become familiar to her in the past few days. The blonde child smiled to herself as she bounced around in the weeds, trying to capture the grasshoppers that stayed just ahead of her. In one hand she grasped a jar in which a few insects were held captive, and with the other she snatched a large brown grasshopper.

"Gotcha," she announced triumphantly.

Ashley followed the child as she jumped around, her full attention on capturing the bugs. Ashley noticed that the child drew ever closer to the forest that surrounded the grounds. She sensed that from the covering of the woods and brush, someone was watching the child with an enthusiasm of a completely different kind. A darker kind.

Gretchen bent to pluck a grasshopper from the weeds. She saw the big shoes first, and then the paint-splattered pant legs of the overalls. A quiver of apprehension crossed her face as she looked up to see the person standing before her.

Ashley strained to see the person's features, but they were obliterated by the oversized hat and the beating sun.

Ashley began to fight as though a thousand devils were holding her down. Her heart raced. Catherine jumped from her spot and tried to subdue her.

Somewhere deep inside the image, Ashley struggled, trying to free herself. She had allowed herself to get too close to the child and now they seemed to become one. Ashley could hear Gretchen's thoughts, feel her fear. The tall man had plucked the child off the ground just as she had just seconds before plucked a grasshopper off its leaf. She fought with her life, but the person who held her was much stronger. A horrible-smelling rag was shoved into her face. Within seconds, Ashley/Gretchen began to feel herself blacking out. Time passed. The minds that had been one gradually separating, each withdrawing to their own individual worlds.

After a while, Ashley felt someone stroking her hair. Her face was hot and she was sweating.

"I think that she's coming around." Catherine's voice was far away.

Patricia was saying, "Teri, we know that she's alive. We'll find out what happened to her, and more importantly, where she's gone."

Ashley moaned and opened her eyes slowly. For a moment her mind was fuzzy and she was unsure how she had managed to get into Catherine's arms. She cherished it and allowed herself another moment, though she knew she was fooling herself.

"I'm all right," she said, rising to her knees. She felt embarrassed. She could only imagine what kind of scene she had made. This was the primary reason she feared her powers. Her head pounded as though she had spent the last three days drinking and was now coming down.

Emily asked, "So, what did you see?"

Ashley frowned, remembering. "Gretchen was taken by somebody. I couldn't see his face, but I have a strange feeling she knows him. I know she's still alive. Somewhere."

Teri let her breath out slowly, as if she hadn't realized that she'd been holding it inside her. She wore an expression of relief as she listened to Ashley's description of the incident she'd witnessed.

"There is something else. Whoever took your daughter is close to you, knows you Teri. I sensed that Gretchen knew him too and that he caused her a great deal of fear. There's more." Ashley looked from face to face in the sober silence that filled the room. "I got this feeling that Gretchen wasn't the first child he's taken, but she may be the last. Something's interrupted his plans. Something he didn't count on, but she's not safe. Time is an issue. We have to find Gretchen soon. Very soon."

Catherine put her hands up as if to stop a physical confrontation. "Look, we're getting in way over our heads here. I don't think that this house was ever filled with anything but pain and hurt. Plus, a child had disappeared. I'm not going to say that the two are connected — that would be absurd. But I think that we should get the police involved in this. It could have been someone working on renovating the house, but Gretchen's been kidnapped and that's police business. I'm beginning to wonder if we should just fold up the whole mission here and go home."

Patricia shook her head. "Not a chance in your life that I'm going home now. Whatever we woke up here will follow us to the end of time unless we resolve it here. We know too much to turn back now. As far as the child is concerned, I think Emily and Teri should go to the police tomorrow and lay it on the line about what we know."

After what felt like hours of arguing back and forth about their next plan of action, they all agreed in the end to stick with the investigation a little longer.

Ashley sat with a piece of paper and a pen on the window seat in her room. Looking out toward the ocean, she was deep in thought when she heard a soft knock on her door. "Come in," she called, laying aside the pad.

Catherine opened the door and peered in. "We ordered out and got some Chinese food. Are you hungry?"

Ashley gestured for her to enter. "I was just sitting here thinking about a few things. Mostly about the dreams and the different things we know about the house."

"Which isn't much," Catherine said, sitting opposite Ashley on the wide window seat.

Ashley nodded in agreement. "But," she said, handing the pad of paper to Catherine, "I made a list of things that might help us to get to the bottom of this whole mess."

She slid next to Catherine and was overcome by the scent of her perfume. She felt intoxicated for a moment. Ashley consciously forced her feelings away and concentrated on the list.

"Here's the way I see it," she began. "We know about the fruit cellar. We know the woman kept a diary and that her sister was named Margaret. We know that there was some dark secret that sent a wedge straight down the fabric of the family. We know that the older man — I assume he's the father — was murdered in the study by someone."

Catherine reread the list before she said, "Perhaps that's why the spirits can't rest here. Maybe he's calling for you to solve his murder?"

Ashley shook her head. "I have a feeling it goes a lot deeper than that. I just can't seem to grasp the missing link."

" I think you're right. There must be more to this than we know. I have this feeling there's something else surrounding the death of the father that you can't see in your dreams. I think that more than one person died."

"We need to move quickly. It feels like all hell's going to break loose. I have to admit, I'm a bit scared of what could happen. You know, I can't tell you what's going to happen, I just have this feeling that there's danger here. Nobody's safe." Ashley looked down at the floor. She hoped she didn't sound foolish — especially to Catherine, her secret love.

Catherine shivered. "What do you mean? Who's in danger?"

Ashley shuddered. She could hear the words forming in her head and tried to bring them to her mouth. Finally, she sighed and looked Catherine in the eye. "I am."

CHAPTER NINE

For the first night in years, Ashley did not dream — or if she did, she did not remember. When she woke, however, she felt like she hadn't slept at all. Her body ached from her head to her feet. Her mind was fuzzy and her thoughts went fleeting by like messages she couldn't hear.

She groaned and pushed the sheets back. It was then she discovered why her body complained. Her feet were caked with dried mud. Cuts and bruises marred her legs as though she had spent the entire night climbing the rocky cliffs that brooded over the ocean just beyond the old, stately mansion.

Fear shot through her. Her hands were covered with blood. A scream welled up in her throat, but she forced it back down. There was an explanation for this, she reasoned.

She jumped from her bed and ran for the door of the bedroom, then stopped short. On the other side she heard voices. Odd, she thought. These were voices she didn't recognize outside of her dreams. For a moment, she thought she *was* dreaming. She took a quick look around her room and found nothing out of the ordinary.

"I don't know what to tell you, Charles," a man said in soft tones. "She will heal, but what she was doing out there on a night like this is beyond me. She's got some bumps and bruises that will heal with time, but . . ." He paused.

"But, what," another voice said with a coldness that Ashley recognized immediately.

"She's two months pregnant. I don't think she could possibly be a fit mother. I think she's gone around the bend, so to speak. When I saw her she was mumbling incoherently about such things that I dare not repeat professionally. Have you thought about having her committed? You know, to a place where her illness can be taken care of? Also, someplace where her child can be taken care of, you know, before it is born."

"I thank you, doctor, for coming all this way to tend to Rebecca, but such family matters I am not prepared to discuss with you. If you will let me know what your bill will be, I will pay now before you take leave. And I am willing to pay you for your long ride out here in this weather. Of course, you will not be discussing this matter with anyone else and there will be no record of this visit, if you understand my meaning here, Doctor Evans." Ashley heard the voice fade as the footsteps disappeared down the hallway.

She puzzled over the meaning of the conversation when suddenly the door opened a crack, and then wider. A small woman who seemed frail and old stepped into the room. She shut the door quietly behind her. The woman's face was pinched with worry, making her look even older.

"Oh, Becky, my Becky. My poor child," the woman whispered softly, her gaze on the bed.

Ashley turned with surprise. Lying on her bed was the same young woman she had seen in her dreams of the fruit cellar. She marveled at the similarity between herself and the youngster in the bed. They could have been sisters. And the thing that stumped her the most was how much the woman looked like her mother.

As the old woman approached her ailing daughter, the image slowly began to fade until Ashley was left staring at the floral patterned sheets.

Emily woke in the arms of her lover. She stretched and yawned as she came fully awake. It wasn't until the fog cleared from her mind that she realized that she was being watched with some intensity. She sat up quickly and focused on the figure standing at the foot of the bed.

A starched white apron around her waist, a woman stood wringing her hands. Against the apron her large, black hands never stopped moving. The woman looked behind her as though she were aware that she had only a few minutes in a place that was off-limits to her.

When she spoke, her deep voice shook with apprehension. "You've got to help us, Missy. He comin' back for what's his. He won't stop, no sir, not till you all dead. He waited and called for a long time and he gonna take us all with him when he come. You've got to help us."

Suddenly, a chill filled the room and a look of fear crossed the woman's face. She turned and hurried out the door.

The next thing Emily knew, she was holding Teri and hiding under the covers. The bed was shaking and she could hear tables and chairs crashing into the wall, the tinkle of breaking glass.

Catherine woke to the feeling of being shaken almost straight out of her bed. At first, all she saw was blackness, then she gasped.

A nun with pleading eyes stood in front of her. Her habit was torn and muddy. The cloth had turned from a starched white to a dull brown. She looked as though she had walked through the worst terrain in a storm.

Catherine squeezed her eyes shut. When she opened them again, the woman remained where she stood. Her eyes still pleading from under her wimple and veil. Catherine did not feel fear, but rather, pity. She moved to say something, but the woman spoke first.

"I know where to find the child you seek. The time is growing short. All will perish if you remain here. His time is coming."

Catherine, mystified, questioned the apparition. "Where is she? And who is the man you're talking about? Who are you?"

A worried look crossed the face of the shadowy nun. "I'm Mary Margaret," she said before she faded to the world from which she came. Then she repeated her warning: "Time is growing short."

Patricia stood in front of the old vanity mirror and was applying the last touches of her eye liner when from the very edge of the mirror she caught an image of a woman. Her mouth went dry. The woman could have been her double. She whirled around, thinking her mind was playing tricks on her.

What she expected to see was not what she saw. The woman moved quietly through the room, the only sound the rustling of her gown. She seemed oblivious as she went about her own affairs. Patricia watched with fascination.

The woman's hair was down around her shoulders and spilled halfway down her back. It was smooth and glossy as if she had just finished brushing it before bed. The long white gown she wore seemed almost two sizes too big for her petite, slight body.

When the woman disappeared into the huge walk-in closet, Patricia heard what sounded like wood scraping on wood. Soon, she returned with a book. She went to the door and fixed the lock on it.

From the desk, the woman took out an inkwell

and a fountain pen. She sat down in the glow of an oil lamp and wrote in the book.

Patricia turned quickly to the sound of Emily's voice booming in the hallway. When she turned again, the woman had vanished.

"What in the name of tarnation is going on," Patricia asked herself.

"That's it," Emily declared angrily in the hallway. "I've had it. One way or another, I'm getting to the bottom of this."

Patricia was the first to her door. Emily stood there in her red Kimono in the hall. Her face was flushed with anger. "What in the love of grace is the matter with you?"

Emily bristled. "I've had it with this house. I have just spent the last five minutes in the worst case of poltergeist-haunting ever. Our room is a mess. Go in there and look for yourselves, if you don't believe me." Her gaze moved from one face to the next.

Ashley found her words to be false. The room was in perfect order. Nothing seemed to be disturbed at all except the bed coverings, which were all over the floor. Ashley guessed that whatever happened, it scared the wits out of Emily. She chuckled inside. The place was getting to all of them. She would almost give credit to hysteria, except she remembered what had happened to herself that morning.

"Em, nothing's been disturbed in here," Ashley said with a straight face.

Emily turned on her heels. Obviously angry at the insinuation, she peered into her room. She turned to Teri. "Please tell me you saw something going on in there. My God, it was loud enough to wake the dead."

Patricia smiled. "I'm afraid that whatever happened, the dead are awake. I had a visit from a friend this morning."

Catherine nodded, "I did too. Someone named Sister Mary Margaret came to see me, to warn me. She said that she knows where the child is." She glanced at Teri and added, "I don't know if she meant Gretchen."

Emily still looked like she was ready to take on the whole host of phantoms roaming the house.

"I know what Teri and I saw in that bedroom. It looked like a shit storm of furniture, luggage and clothes. Everything was destroyed and lying in heaps by the time it was all over."

Teri chimed in. "It was real. And now look at it. Just as calm and peaceful as if nothing had happened at all."

"All I know," Catherine said, "is that I was offered a warning of sorts. 'Get out before he comes.' "

"That's what I was told. By a black woman who was dressed like she was the housemaid or something. She was frightened. She told me more or less the same thing. Get out before it's too late for all of us." Emily relayed the details calmly.

"I'm afraid that was what me and the Mrs. were told on several occasions," a man said from behind them.

Emily jumped, startled for a moment until the fact registered in her mind that he was human and very real.

"Mr. Dupree, you scared the mother of Jesus out of me," She exclaimed.

Dupree took the matchstick he was chewing on from his mouth. "Well, I knocked, hoping to get Teri to the door." He glared at the woman until she slipped off into the bedroom. Emily had noticed before that he was less than civil to Teri, and she wondered why. "I hope you're finding the accommodations comfortable, madam." He squinted in disapproval.

Emily decided she could not ignore his rude innuendos. She smiled and glanced toward the bedroom. "Yes, I'm finding things very comfortable here, thank you."

With this Dupree nodded, looking stern. "If you'll excuse me, I'll make myself come coffee in the kitchen. When you ladies are ready, I'll meet you there to find out how things are going." He smiled at Patricia as if to say he was sorry she had to put up with this. "Ma'am," he said to her, then found his way down the stairs.

Catherine was the first dressed and down the stairs. She was fighting with the gold chain from which hung a Black Hills gold cross when she stopped short in her tracks. On the other side of the double, swinging kitchen doors, an argument was in full swing. Dupree and Teri seemed to be locked in combat.

"Your mother said, 'Oh, please John, give her one more chance. I'm sure she's changed since the Lord punished her.' And I said to myself, oh no, not her. She'll never change. So what do I do? Like a fool I give you another chance and this is how you pay me back," Dupree bellowed.

"You and your damned religious ways. You don't know anything, Dad, you never have. You'rer too God damned stubborn to see things the way that they are. I don't want to be with a man. It's as simple as that. It won't change, it's not a disease, and I'm not sinning." Teri's voice was low, reasoning.

"What about Gretchen?" Dupree asked with concern.

"What about her," Teri spat, her words coated with venom.

"Well, she must want to be with her daddy."

"Gretchen was an accident. I never wanted to be with him. I've told you and Mother this a dozen times."

"You went out with the boy, you must have liked him. You got yourself in the family way," Dupree accused her, his voice rising again.

"I never 'dated' Randy Taylor, Dad. You want the truth, I was raped. I was raped by the nice Taylor boy. Just leave me alone." Teri sobbed.

Catherine moved away from the door, feeling as though she were intruding on something very private. She had already heard too much. Quickly, she tiptoed out of the dining room and into the entrance hall. Her nerves didn't calm down until she breathed the warm morning air.

* * * * *

83

Glancing out her window, Ashley caught a glimpse of Catherine walking toward the large barn that still stood on a shaky foundation.

She hit the stairs two at a time and almost ran into Mr. Dupree coming out of the dining room. " 'Scuse me," Ashley said brightly.

Dupree mumbled something about coming back later and went out the front door with a crisp slam.

" 'Scuse me," Ashley said again, sarcastically this time.

She went outside and followed the trail past the barn to the edge of the forest. She froze for a moment, remembering the fear of the child. Slowly, she shook it off and slipped into the shelter of the forest.

Sparrows and woodpeckers chirped in the arms of the trees. Seagulls cried as they fished in the still pools where high tide had abandoned small marine animals. The spray off of the ocean smelled sweet and fresh. Ashley enjoyed being near the water. She marveled, with envy, the power of the ocean at high tide, and likewise envied the stillness and peace after the fury. She hugged herself, reveling in the few moments that she could spend alone with nature.

Too soon, she found herself at the partial ruins of what looked like a convent. Most of it lay in the rubble of stones and wooden rafters. The only portion still standing seemed to be the chapel. Carefully, Ashley negotiated a path between and around the huge chunks of rock and wall. She figured that this must be where Catherine had disappeared to.

The door that once had led from the chapel to the outside was missing. Ashley stood in the archway and peered in. The only light inside the chapel came from the stained glass windows that reached almost from the floor to the ceiling on the far side. At first, she didn't see anything, and then she caught sight of movement from deep within.

"Catherine," she called from the entry way, unsure about going inside the ancient building.

"Here."

Ashley moved carefully through the doorway, the floorboards squeaking and complaining under her weight. She made her way to the end of a long division of pews. She called, "Catherine."

Smiling, Catherine stepped out of the shadows.

"What are you doing here?" Ashley asked, moving closer.

Catherine shrugged. "Just looking around. What are *you* doing here? Are you following me or something?"

Ashley thought about denying it. "Yes. I was being nosy; I wanted to see what you were up to."

"I see," Catherine said, smiling.

"So, what are you doing?"

"I was just curious. After seeing Sister Mary Margaret and all I thought that I might be able to sense her better in the place she used to live."

Ashley nodded. It made sense to her. "Find anything?"

"Well," Catherine said, dusting off her hands, "see that balcony up there? Enclosed with that mesh?"

Ashley followed Catherine's gaze to the upper balcony that hung over the pews at the rear of the chapel. She wondered how sound the floorboards were, and for how long the convent and chapel had been unoccupied. She guessed that the floor was probably rotted, especially if the place had been empty for a long time.

"That's where the nuns sat when they came to mass." What looked like a painful memory flashed across Catherine's face.

"Did you pick that up psychically?" Ashley asked sincerely.

Catherine crossed her arms. "No. When I was a nun, the convent where I lived had been renovated to a degree, but the old chapel had the same kind of balcony. A long time ago, when they started building convents away from the motherhouse, they'd build a chapel so the lay people from the towns could come and worship. The nuns sat separated from the congregation — depending, of course on which order the nuns belonged to."

"I see," Ashley said, though she didn't.

Catherine laughed. "It's very confusing, I know. But that's the way it was. Still is in some places. Some orders aren't ever permitted any contact with the world at all."

To Ashley, the idea of never seeing her mother and her family drove her crazy. She couldn't imagine living with a bunch of women and having contact with only them for the rest of her life.

As if sensing Ashley's thoughts, Catherine laughed again, a sound like soft summer rain. Ashley longed to touch her once more, if only for a moment. But she knew that she'd only want more and try greedily to get what she wanted. An emotion stirred deep within her.

Catherine touched her on the elbow. "It's a very holy thing. Only certain people are called to that kind of life."

Ashley asked, "What about you? What type of convent did you belong to?"

"My community's mission was teaching and nursing. They go to Africa, South America, certain parts of the United States. They work with the poor mostly. It's hard work. I got to go to Africa for six months. I liked to teach. I didn't want to be in a cloistered order, where you serve the world mainly through prayer."

"Oh," Ashley said, nodding. She still couldn't see anyone sit in a room and pray all day. She loved her freedom too much to give it up. "So then, was our Sister Mary Margaret cloistered?"

"I think they were a teaching order. That would explain such a large building for what I believe was a very small community of women."

"So why is this nun haunting the mansion? Aren't nuns suppose to be the first ones accepted in the afterlife?"

Catherine laughed. "Nuns are people, my friend. They're no holier than the rest of us just because they take the veil. Nobody's perfect. Just because a woman is vowed doesn't mean she'll be at peace in the next life. But, I think that either our friend has been sent as a warning to us, or that she's going after something she couldn't finish in this life."

"Well, it's clear that she was trying to warn you about something. And it seems that whatever it is, we aren't going to like it much. But you think she's searching for something? Searching for what?" Ashley followed Catherine from the threshold into the bright sunlight.

Catherine shrugged. "I think she was murdered. Maybe she's seeking the life she lost so suddenly. She knows she's dead, but I think that she can't rest until someone, somewhere, ferrets out the truth behind her death and her life. She seems to be surrounded by darkness. Secrets."

"I sense that the whole damned family is surrounded by secrets and half-truths. I mean, a nun who's murdered. A child who's half nuts and takes to venturing out at all hours of the night, doing Lord knows what. A father who's beyond cruel and bizarre, and a mother who seems to be trapped in the middle of a nightmare that she has no power to stop. What the hell went on around here?" Ashley asked as they wended their way down the stone path that wound around to the front of the convent.

She found herself back where she had entered, where the wall had crumbled. She turned casually to say something else, when she saw Catherine digging furiously in the ground.

Ashley knelt down next to her. "Was it something I said?"

Catherine was clearly in no mind to be humored. "There's something here. Deep in the ground. I can feel it. I tried to walk away, but I couldn't move. There's something here, and I bet it belonged to Sister Mary Margaret."

"Okay. Let me help." Ashley began tearing away at the sod. "Just calm down. If it's here, we'll find it." She glanced up and noticed that they were kneeling almost directly in front of what was once the huge abbey. Only the stately wooden doors and part of one wall were left standing. The gray stone looked cold and forbidding all of a sudden. Ashley wished the walls could speak, could tell her what had happened so many years ago.

From a hole a half-foot deep and about ten inches wide, they found what they had been searching for. Catherine handled the rosary as reverently as if the Pope himself had given it to her.

The beads were caked with layers of dirt. Amazingly, the pieces stayed intact, despite the years it had been buried in the soil. The entire rosary was made from large, wooden beads and a wooden cross with a crude piece of metal that had probably represented the crucifixion. That it hadn't disintegrated astounded Ashley, and she watched as Catherine fingered the beads.

From the moment that Catherine touched it, the rosary seemed to come alive in her hands. She began to see things in her mind about the woman who had owned it for so long. She began to sense the pain and desperation that the young woman had gone through. She could feel the anger, humility, and the hate.

Finally, she began to sense something joyous. Love. The woman had felt love for someone and Catherine guessed that that love belonged to the dark-skinned woman, the dark-skinned woman she had seen the day before in her vision. The lightheartedness of love was the strongest sensation, coming through the beads like a storm rushing in from the ocean. It must have been, Catherine thought, the last thing Margaret felt before she died.

"Oh, my God," she muttered, holding the beads close to her heart. Tears formed in her eyes. "She was going to meet her lover the night that she died."

Ashley put her arm around Catherine and pulled her close.

Patricia sat on her bed, looking around her room. Her mind was whirling with thoughts of the woman she had seen, the woman who looked just like her. Curious, she got up and opened the doors to the large, old closet and studied the interior. On her knees, her reading glasses propped on her nose, she examined every plank of wood that ran across the floor, every seam between the planks. She knew what she was looking for, but it seemed to elude her.

Taking the miniature flashlight that she always kept packed in her suitcase, she crawled deeper into the closet, going slowly from wall to wall, looking for imperfections in the boards. Nothing. Damn, she thought. As she began backing out of the closet, suddenly one of the boards bent slightly under her knee.

Ah-hah, she thought. In the middle of the closet was a board that could be pried up. It took her several minutes to jimmy it out, but when it was free, she knew she had found her treasure — a journal, with a thick cover front and back.

With the joy that children feel on Easter, having found the eggs painstakingly hidden by parents, Patricia opened the book. The pages were yellowed with age, and she feared the information contained inside would crumble. Very carefully, she eased the cover open. On the first page was the date, written in a precise and flowing hand, though very small.

April 12, 1891.

Greedily, Patricia read on.

Charles came home drunk again tonight. He announced to the children and I that we are to pack anything and everything that we value, as we are leaving Charleston immediately. I tried to ask why, but you know him when he gets into these moods, Lord Jesus. He struck me with his fist and told me never to question him again. I am afraid of leaving him. He says that we are destined for God's country, wherever that is. He says that we are going West to a place near Portland, Oregon. We'll be leaving everything that Poppa left me, not that it was much after the war, Lord knows, the Yankees did not leave us much. Though, over the years, we have returned it to the grandeur it once was.

Charles has acted quite strangely since coming home from the last meeting with those men last month. He seems to have gotten more and more angry, not that he was ever much of a husband. In reality, he's gotten worse. From the time that we lost Charles Jr. last summer, he has gotten moodier. The accident changed him. Lately, I have worried about his fascination with the North. All of the promises of quick profit that seem to be floating around these days have got me wondering if he has fallen into some sort of compromise.

Whatever happens, my sweet Lord, watch over my children and I assure You we will not fall into any evils that may beset us in the future. I cannot help but feel that only death will come from this move to the North, and I am chilled with the thoughts that come to my mind. At least Rinee has agreed to come with me. Lord, I cannot see my life without her there. She seems to be my only friend these days, and I thank You for her.

Judith Ann Lillian Winslow.

Patricia turned to the end of the book. The last entry was dated July, 1896. She held in her hands a diary of almost three carefully recorded years. The life of an unhappy woman, Patricia thought. She suspected that some of the answers she sought were in this book. She gingerly closed the journal and laid it on the bed next to her. For a long moment, she chewed on the end of her reading glasses, in deep thought.

The child Gretchen stirred slowly awake. She felt as though she had been sleeping for a lifetime. Her ankle throbbed in pain, and she realized that she had fallen asleep with the ankle bracelet tight against her skin. She moved slowly as her entire being pulsed as one pain.

She could see a shaft of light beaming in from where she had opened a small hole in the wall, all the way to the outside. This way she could see outside, keep cool, and breathe. The problem was the nights were getting colder now, and she didn't have a blanket, only her old jacket.

From the time that the man had abducted her, she could only remember a few times when her mind was clear. One of those times she had made the hole in the wall. Another time, she had been certain there were voices coming from the floor below. She had cowered in the corner, expecting the man to come back. She never could really see his face well, since he usually came when it was dark. She shivered with the memory. Whenever the man came, he brought her a little food. When she was finished, he would plunge a needle into her arm and soon she would drift off to sleep. But the last time she heard voices, no one came.

She had begun to dream in clear images of people she didn't know. Somehow she sensed that they were looking for her, and she tried to tell them where she was, but each time, they left her alone in the darkness. When she woke, she figured it was just a dream anyway, and the man was right. Nobody wanted her. Not even her mother. After all, he'd told her, she hadn't come for her, so she must not want her.

More than once, the thought of pounding on the floor or screaming out the tiny air hole crossed her mind. But she was afraid to do it again. The first time she tried that, the man came almost immediately and beat her until she stopped screaming. Since then, she couldn't make her mouth work. The words came to her mind, but she couldn't speak.

Gretchen sighed and pulled her knees up to her chest. She wondered where the man could be. Her stomach rumbled and she knew that it had been at least a couple of days since he had come. Why had he stopped coming? A fear gnawed at her gut. Maybe he was dead. She didn't really care either way about the man, but she knew that if something happened to him, she would surely die inside the tiny room.

At least she had her knife. It was just a butter knife, but she had managed to keep it from one of her first meals. She had been terrified he'd find it missing, but he hadn't even noticed. That was how she'd made the small hole through the wall to the outside. In the beginning, the work had been easy. It was not until she came to the outside wall that she had found some difficulty. The wood was thick and wouldn't give way easily to the knife.

She stretched the chain as far as it would go and peeked out the hole. She couldn't see anything below or above, only the ocean that roared beyond her. She decided she would have to make the hole bigger, without bringing it to the attention of the man — if he was still around. Carefully, she began digging away at the wood, determined to find a way out.

CHAPTER TEN

The women didn't meet again until late in the afternoon. Everyone was buzzing about her discoveries, disappointments and concerns.

Emily rose above the chatter, "First things first, gals. Teri and I went to the police today to report what we had seen."

"How did it go?" Catherine asked, taking her mind off the rosary in her hand.

"Not good." Emily sighed. "The detective in charge of Gretchen's case just about laughed us out of his office."

"Did you put it to him gracefully? I mean, you didn't say that a bunch of us psychically picked up on Gretchen, did you?" Ashley sat with a steaming mug of coffee in front of her.

"Of course I didn't. I have more sense than that you know. I told him that, well, that . . . All right, I told him that I sensed what had happened to Gretchen. What was I supposed to say?" Emily scowled, clearly still angry.

"So, we're back to square one." Teri was close to tears.

"Buck up, hon, we'll find her," Patricia reassured her warmly.

"Yes," Emily said, nodding. "We will. Apparently there've been several children who have come up missing in the past few months. The police suspect that Gretchen may fit in with all of those other cases, so she's kinda stuffed in with all the rest."

After a moment, Patricia laid the journal on the table and declared, "Well, girls, I seem to have something of interest to our little investigation here."

"What's that?" Ashley asked coming next to her mother. "It looks a lot like the book I saw in the dream. Don't tell me you found the infamous fruit cellar?"

"Nope." Patricia grinned. "But I found Judith Ann Lillian Winslow's journal. It appears that she kept one for most of her life, but this is the last one, the only one I could find."

"I assume Judith is the mother," Catherine said, touching the cover of the book. She could get no impressions off of it.

Patricia grinned again. "Indeed. From what I've

read so far, the father's name was Charles Winslow, Senior, and he was not a nice man. According to Judith, he was quite a rogue. He drank too much, and gambling kept him out at all hours of the night and day. Not to mention his running around with other women. On a whim, he moved his family out here from South Carolina to be closer to his sister. At least that's how Judith understood it. I have a feeling there were other underlying reasons."

"His sister?" Catherine asked with curiosity.

"His sister was the mother superior at the convent across the way. Their missionary school educated the Indian children for a while and then the children of the town. It seems that Charles was always quite fond of his sister and decided to follow her out here — how do I say this — to see to her needs. The Winslow family was quite wealthy and remained so even after the Civil War." Patricia was browsing through the journal.

"So now we're starting to get some substance to the whos and whats around here," Emily said as she held Teri's hand.

"I've never heard anything about the Winslows," Teri said, "other than that the entire family disappeared the same night the convent burned to the ground. Rumor had it that it was God's judgment on the Winslows and that the convent harbored terrible secrets. Nobody talks about it anymore."

Catherine set the rosary gently on the table. "Ashley and I found this outside the front of the convent this morning. Sister Mary Margaret was murdered. I sensed that by touching her rosary. She was on her way to meet her lover when she was pushed off the side of the cliff. She fell to her death on the rocks below. Her lover was the daughter of the only servant woman here."

Catherine looked down, fingering the rosary. The information seemed to be coming together. Some of their questions were answered, but the most important ones were still troubling. Who murdered Sister Mary Margaret and her father? What did Charles Winslow want now after all these years, and why would the Winslows follow with such vigor the Windlow family for generations? Were there other dark secrets hidden within the walls of the big house?

Ashley knew she was dreaming again as she watched the child sleep. This time the child seemed younger than before. Moonbeams shone through the window and filled the room with eerie shadows.

Ashley wondered about the meaning of this dream. Usually the child was in the fruit cellar, and she was older.

She crossed the room slowly. The girl was in the throes of a nightmare and she moaned hauntingly in her sleep. Ashley longed to comfort her, but she knew that her hands were not real.

Rebecca, Ashley thought. That was her name.

Suddenly, the child's eyes opened in horror. Beads of sweat rolled down her forehead and neck, soaking the front of her gown. For a long moment, the child seemed to be looking at nothing, seeing nothing, and then she blinked. The muscles around her mouth relaxed slightly. Audibly, she sighed.

Rebecca snuggled down under the heavy blankets on the bed, and tried to shrink under the covers. Ashley watched with detached curiosity.

The knob on the door turned slowly. Ashley sensed the fear that loomed around the child. Rebecca breathed heavily, pulled the covers up around her chin and closed her eyes as if pretending to sleep.

As the door swung open on freshly oiled hinges, the child began to whimper. Her eyes flew open, wide with fear. Ashley watched the figure enter carrying a lamp with a low flame. He shut the door behind him.

Ashley could see his face as he placed the oil lamp on the pedestal near the door. It was Charles Winslow. On his face was a twisted, drunken smile.

Ashley guessed what was going to happen next and she felt the nausea rise in her throat. She looked around the room for something to defend Rebecca with.

Suddenly, she felt herself slipping out from the scene. Rebecca was closing her mind. Sliding into the inner world she'd created to protect herself from the horrible truth. There she wouldn't remember what happened to her those nights as a child. She would recall only one thing — it was not the darkness that was evil, it was what lurked in the darkness.

Ashley woke shortly before dawn. She turned on the bedside lamp to chase the darkness away. Inside, she was shaking and she still felt nauseous. She was filled with anger and revulsion.

She peeled off the covers. Her nightshirt was soaked with perspiration. On shaky knees, she rose from the bed. She felt suddenly alone and frightened, as if she were a child again and monsters were invading the privacy of her room.

In the hallway she stood fighting with herself. Part of her mind begged her to find a safe spot with someone else, but pride kept her from going into her mother's room. She could hear Patricia snoring loudly. Ashley looked toward Catherine's room down the hall. Suddenly, she felt ignorant. After all, it was only a dream, she chided herself, but it was more than a dream. It felt real, like it had really happened to her many years ago.

One thought chased another around and around in her mind. There was no way to stop it now, so why dwell on it? What was there to gain from pursuing it? Why did Rebecca pick her to know the horrid truths, and why did she feel that this was only the tip of the iceberg? Ashley shivered in the darkness of the hall. She could either go back into her room and wait out the night, or wake someone up and talk.

It took Catherine a couple of minutes to realize that someone was knocking at her door. She rose slowly and squinted at the red number on the travel alarm clock. She didn't really comprehend the time. With her slippers on she shuffled to the door.

At first, all she could see was the light of the oil lamp that burned in front of her. Slowly, the figure behind it began to take shape. It was a child who looked no older than ten or eleven. Her long blonde hair fell down past her shoulders. The child's eyes pleaded with her. There was a look of betrayal, pain and anger there . . . and something else that Catherine couldn't quite see. Before she could say a word, the child whispered, "Can I stay here with you tonight, Margaret?"

As Catherine reached for the child, she vanished. It had seemed so real. Catherine shook her head. The flesh-and-blood child had been standing in front of her with tears running down her small face. She could almost feel the fear that surrounded the girl. Something stirred within Catherine, a sensation of being outside of herself, yet within her body. She knew the feeling belonged to Mary Margaret.

When she tried to examine the emotion, it too vanished. She wondered what it all meant, but figured that it somehow must tie in with all the rest.

Ashley looked like hell and Catherine noticed the change immediately. She pulled up a chair and put her hand on Ashley's. "Bad night?"

Ashley forced a smile. "Yeah. I didn't sleep well. I've been up since a little after three."

Concerned, Catherine asked, "Why? Did one of our friends visit you in the night?"

For a long time Ashley wouldn't answer. Catherine was about to forget the question and change the subject when Ashley finally spoke. There was a pleading look in her eyes and it sent chills through her body.

"Something horrible happened last night. I saw things, monstrous things in a dream. There are more secrets in this house than I care to know about anymore. Why don't they just leave me alone? I've had enough. For fifteen years I've been haunted by people I don't even know. I don't care about them. Do you understand what I am saying?" Ashley took a sip from her coffee cup. She looked drained and anxious.

Catherine nodded. She didn't understand fully, yet she tried to comfort her friend. It must have been something more powerful than usual to cause her such anxiety. She didn't want to push Ashley about the dream. In time, she knew Ashley would tell her.

"I had a visitor last night," Catherine said lightly. "It was the littlest one. Rebecca, I guess." She felt the muscles under her hand tense and she saw the strain on Ashley's face. She had unexpectedly hit a nerve.

"Rebecca was in my dream last night, though I hesitate to call it a dream. It was more like being there in person. Is that possible? You know, to go back into the past and witness things that happened in another time?" Ashley asked, finishing her coffee.

"I never used to think so until I came here," Catherine said truthfully.

"I guess it really doesn't matter one way or the other. The things we've experienced here no one would believe anyway." She smiled slightly at the irony of it all. "It seems so real, Catherine, like it was happening to me. I've never been so repulsed in my life."

"What happened," Catherine asked carefully.

"The child was in bed and had just woken from a terrible dream. I was watching her when he came into the room. Charles. I could feel her fear — like she was a part of me and I was a part of her. I knew what was going to happen before it happened, and I know this wasn't the first time. He sat on the edge of the bed for a while. I could smell the whiskey on his breath and the sourness of his body odor. I tried to run, tried to get away, but she wouldn't let me go." Ashley's voice rose hysterically and she began to cry.

Catherine pulled her into her arms and called her name, trying to draw her back to reality, all the while replaying the scenario at the door the night before. Now she understood the vague feeling that had plagued her last night after the child left. She knew what Mary Margaret was trying to tell her. She could understand what Ashley was feeling because she felt it as well.

Emily couldn't believe what she was seeing. She had only seen it once in her life and even then she had thought she was hallucinating. She closed her eyes and opened them slowly, all the while telling herself that it wasn't true. But this time she couldn't deny it. The aura that surrounded Ashley was a muddy brown.

She turned to Patricia. "Do you see anything strange about Ashley this morning?"

Patricia shrugged. "She looks tired." She patted Emily on the arm and motioned her to the kitchen. Teri stood at the stove placing long pieces of bacon in a frying pan. The two women ignored her for the moment. "What's got you bugged?" Patricia asked, pouring herself a cup of coffee.

"I was talking about Ashley's aura. It's light brown. Peek out there and look again."

Patricia frowned, then went to peer out into the dining room.

"Did you see it that time," Emily asked pulling apart a freshly baked cinnamon roll.

"Yes," Patricia said hesitantly. "I guess so."

"Doesn't that concern you?" Without waiting for her to answer, Emily added, "Brown. There is something serious going on. Brown means serious illness — physical or spiritual."

"So what does that mean, exactly?"

Emily brushed the crumbs off of her clothes. "It means that Ashley is somehow dying. But at least it's not black. That's the worst. Right now it is just a light brown. I think that we should get her out of here as soon as possible."

At that moment, Ashley came into the kitchen, followed closely by Catherine.

Ashley went to the point quickly and told the others about her dream the night before. Emily was shocked, but before she could say anything, Ashley said, "I've decided to go back to Portland. I know that I agreed to help, but this has gotten to be too much for me. I can't take it anymore." There was an element of panic in her voice. "I simply have to get out."

Patricia exhaled slowly. "I'll help you get your stuff ready to go. This is probably the best thing for you right now."

Ashley sighed, and Emily could see the pent-up tension leaving her body.

"I'll probably go ahead and leave after breakfast. I wish —" She paused and reached for Emily's hand. "I wish I could stay. But I promise to work from afar. I'll try to find out all I can about the Winslow family. And I'll call the police in Portland — maybe they can do something about finding Gretchen."

Emily smiled and watched Ashley leave. Suddenly, she felt a foreboding that she couldn't shake. Somewhere deep within, she knew that whatever brought Ashley here wouldn't let her go so easily. An overwhelming feeling rose in her chest and tears threatened. She felt defeated.

CHAPTER ELEVEN

Ashley tossed her suitcase into the car and turned back to the old house. She wanted to look at it one more time. On the second floor she saw the face of a woman at the window of her mother's room. At first, Ashley thought it was Patricia, but as she lifted her hand to wave, her mother came out the door in her usual rush.

Ashley turned her attention to the woman again. She still stood there, unmoving, watching her from the second floor. She held a string of beads in her hand. Ashley felt a sickness in the pit of her stomach.

"You forgot your purse, honey," Patricia said, tossing the bag onto the seat. She followed Ashley's gaze to the window on the second floor and shrugged. "Be careful, Ma. Don't push it too hard, you know, it's okay to quit." Ashley slid into the driver's seat and pushed the keys into the ignition.

Angry-looking rain clouds hung over the ocean. Ashley knew that she had better leave soon, otherwise she might not be able to leave at all. She gave her mother one more look before she turned the key in the ignition.

The car refused to start. It refused to turn over. In fact, not even the lights would come on. The battery was dead. Ashley cursed. The panic she had suppressed the entire morning welled up inside of her and threatened to burst.

"What in the world?" Patricia frowned. "Did you leave your lights on or something?"

"Mom, I came up here in the middle of the day. I didn't have the lights on. In fact, I have not been out to my car since we got here. I don't get it." Any other time she could have rationalized it. Explained it away. But this was not any other time.

"Someone'll have jumper cables —"

"Mom, just get the keys to your car. I'll drive it out of here. It's going to storm!" Ashley could hear the desperation in her own voice.

Patricia raced into the house, but as it turned out, none of the cars started. It was futile. Patricia's, Catherine's and Teri's cars were all drained of power. So much for jumper cables.

The wind had picked up, carrying with it the salty spray of the ocean. The storm was very close.

Ashley, by this time, was beside herself. She felt the chilling hands of defeat running down the length of her spine. There was nothing left for her to do. She went to the porch of the mansion, put her head in her hands and cried. She knew that most of what she was feeling was the effects of the dream and the lack of sleep. She was tired, but the thought of sleeping was out of the question.

"I guess you win," she said to no one in particular. Her thoughts turned toward the woman who stood in the second floor window. "You win."

Emily drummed her fingers on the dining room table. A troublesome picture had run through her mind. In the picture, Ashley lay dead on the floor in the study. The lights flickered on and off as a storm raged outside. She saw Catherine crying as she tried to tend to the wounds on Ashley's still body.

The faces around her reflected the general helplessness she felt inside. Emily's blood ran cold as she remembered them trying to start their cars.

Finally she announced, "I can't stand just sitting here like a bunch of dumb ducks on a pond waiting for the hunter. We need to be prepared. We need to arm ourselves. The more we know about the former occupants of this house the better."

"So what do you propose we do?" Catherine asked. "I'm willing to do just about anything at this point."

"I'm going to look for that stupid fruit cellar. It

seems to be the key thing in Ashley's dreams, so there must be something there that we need to know." Emily turned to leave, making a mental note of the things she'd take with her.

"It's coming down in sheets out there. You'll be lucky if you don't drown," Ashley said frankly.

Emily snapped, "It's better than sitting here and not doing anything. If we give up, we won't have a chance to win. I'm not about to give up on you, this investigation, Gretchen, nothing. If you want to, you can sit there on the pity pot, but I'm not." Emily stormed out of the room. After a few moments, Patricia followed.

Gretchen felt the tightness in her stomach. She had gone beyond hunger to another realm. Her stomach would stop complaining, for the most part, until she let the thought of hamburgers and french fries enter her mind. She slept more often and for longer durations. She wasn't sure anymore how many days had passed since the last time she dug and chipped away at the wood of the far wall. Something inside of her warned that if she didn't get out of this place soon, she would die. The thought drove her on.

Her strength had long since left her and she couldn't work on the hole without tiring. She knew that eventually she'd have no more energy for the project. But for now she counted each sliver of dislodged wood as a triumph.

She could hear the rain beating down on the roof above her. She wondered if it would crash in on her. It made her thirsty. She ripped a piece of cloth from her shirt and shoved it through the hole. The rain was blowing at just the right angle and soaked the fabric in a few seconds. Thirstily, she squeezed the water down her parched throat, sucking the cloth. Somewhere in the back of her mind she heard her mother's voice telling her to drink slowly to prevent cramps. She slowed down. The water tasted good and it filled her stomach.

She soaked the cloth again and drank some more. With the metal knife in hand she went back to chipping away at the wall. She had almost made a hole big enough to put her head through.

At first, she thought that she was hearing things, like she so often did these days, so she waited and strained to hear. She pressed her head against the hole. There were voices outside. Two women. And one sounded like her mother. She pushed her head into the hole, hoping to get a glimpse of the outside.

It was not dark yet, but overcast. Through the sheets of rain that came down, she strained to see the two figures that stood in the rain. Both wore dark raincoats with the hoods fastened tightly. Before long, someone arrived wearing a bright yellow raincoat and a funny-looking hat. She could not see their faces. Who were they, and why didn't they come up to give her any food?

The women spoke loudly over the sounds of the storm that raged on around them. Then she heard it. She would have known that voice in the dark. It was her mother. With every bit of strength in her body, Gretchen spoke. She muttered the word out of the hole and into the rain that hurled itself against the wall.

"Momma." It came out as barely a whisper.

Sobbing, Gretchen watched as the women moved away, down the trail that she now recognized from the faded memory deep inside her failing mind. She fell into a heap next to the hole and dropped off immediately into a restless sleep.

Soaking their pants up to their knees, Emily, Patricia and Teri traipsed through the weeds. They had planned on making as many sweeps as necessary until they found the underground cellar. The fruit cellar could be flush to the ground or it could be slightly raised at an angle. It could have doors on it, or the doors could have rotted away through the years, leaving a yawning pit.

For close to two hours they searched. They had only a few unexplored pieces left. Emily could read the dismay on her friend's faces. While the conversation had been strong and positive at the beginning, now it lagged and faded off into silence. Doubts began to creep in. Perhaps the whole thing was an illusion, or the result of mass hysteria. It happened sometimes even with the very best in the business, and after all, they were all amateurs in their own fields.

They had no fancy instruments, training or specialized cameras the professional parapsychologists used so often in their trades. All they had were their unique and special talents.

Emily wondered to herself if it would be enough. As she was trying to console herself, she suddenly felt herself falling. She let out a tiny scream before she hit the bottom.

Patricia and Teri scrambled around the opening Emily had fallen into. Teri called, "Are you all right?"

Emily pulled herself up slowly. Nothing hurt. She felt fortunate. She looked at the rotten pieces of wood laying around on the hard, earthen floor. There were no large splinters of wood she could have fallen on. She sighed. "I'm fine."

On the ground near her feet, Emily found the flashlight and pushed the button. With the narrow beam of light, she found the stairs leading out of the hole.

"Girls," she announced, "I think we found Ashley's fruit cellar."

Teri followed Patricia down the stairs, careful not to trip on the pieces of wood that laid scattered on the earthen stairs.

"My God," Teri breathed, "All of these years and I never knew this was here. I imagine if the teenagers knew about this place they would have thrown their parties down here rather than out there." She gestured over her shoulder.

"This is a hell of a lot more than a fruit cellar," Patricia said, shining her light down the hallway. It seemed larger than Ashley had described. It did indeed seem more like a once-habitable dwelling.

"Well, shall we?" Emily started apprehensively down the hall. The others followed slowly. Along either side of the earthen hallway there had been places cut out of the hard-packed earth for oil lamps. Each little crevice still held the glass lamps, empty now.

The long narrow passage came to an end and veered to the left. Emily probed her mind for the description that Ashley had given. It seemed to her that there should have been two small rooms cut out at either side of the passageway. For the moment, she concerned herself with the room off to the left.

She didn't realize how close behind her the other women were until she stopped abruptly. Patricia almost ran into her and Teri kicked Patrica's shoe.

"What is it?" Patricia asked, obviously spooked by the sudden stop.

"I found the room Ashley told us about, but you're not going to like it," Emily said tersely.

Patricia's voice was shaky. "What?"

"Umm, maybe you'd better come around me and see for yourself," Emily stepped aside so that Teri and Patricia could get a look.

The three of them shined their flashlights into the room. At the far wall was a bed big enough for two people to fit comfortably. At the foot of the bed was a stack of neatly folded blankets ready to stave off the winter chill. The bed itself was covered with a warm-looking comforter and there were feather pillows at the head. It looked perfectly normal, with two exceptions: the bed was in a fruit cellar and the remains of a human body lay in the bed.

Patricia gasped. Teri stood dumbfounded in the doorway. Neither of them seemed sure of what to do next, so Emily pushed into the room, and seemed to break the spell. Even then, they stayed behind Emily as though they feared that the corpse would rise from the bed.

As she drew closer, Emily saw the blonde hair still smoothed out on the pillow. Time had decayed the flesh away but left the fine hair intact. It appeared that the remains were of a woman, for the careworn white gown was buttoned at the throat. Around the neck was a tiny gold cross and the hands clutched a Holy Bible.

Suddenly, Emily felt the small hairs on the back of her neck prickle like they always did before any type of supernatural phenomenon. She didn't want to turn around for she half-suspected what was waiting for her. She wondered if Patricia and Teri felt it too. The eerie presence of another.

Without turning her head, she asked, "Pat, do you feel it?" All she got was an "Uh-huh" from her. She could feel Patricia's fingers digging into her arm. Her mind started to whirl with the worst possible scenarios. She thought she could wait out the visitor, but as the seconds turned into minutes she realized that the spirit had the benefit of the rest of eternity to wait.

Slowly, she turned on her heel. Patricia and Teri followed her cue, and she guessed that she had been elected to act as the shield for them.

"You know," Catherine said after the trio had left the house, "I think Emily's probably right. We need enough information to defend ourselves if it comes down to some sort of a war. And from the way that it looks now, it wouldn't surprise me in the least."

Ashley was barely listening.

"Maybe a good place to start is that journal Pat found. What do you think?" She touched Ashley softly on the hand.

Ashley pulled away.

Ashley found her sanity gradually returning to her

with each second that ticked away in which no horrible vision came to haunt her. She knew that there would be no way she could sleep alone when the lights went out. She wondered who would be there with her when sleep finally became inevitable.

Her thoughts kept twirling, and soon she couldn't hear what Catherine was saying at all. She wondered if the others had found the fruit cellar yet. The fruit cellar that she had convinced herself was only in her mind. Perhaps the dreams meant something else entirely. Perhaps Freud was right about dreams, she thought, they are windows into the mind, into the soul. Maybe she was just going crazy and there was nothing at the house after all. Just a lot of dust, old furniture and memories from the past.

She had almost convinced herself when she again felt Catherine's hand on her own. In an instant, she was yanked back into reality. Ashley couldn't keep herself from falling in deeper love with Catherine, and every touch hurt her more and more.

Ashley smiled. "The journal. Right, the journal. Didn't she leave it in the sitting room? Maybe it would help us find out more about the insanity that went on here." She rose from the table and stole a glance at Catherine. She was embarrassed and wished she could explain everything that was inside of her. But she knew it wouldn't change their circumstances.

Catherine opened the journal to the page where Patricia had left off. She read aloud while Ashley stood at the window and watched the storm blowing in from the ocean.

Today is the first day that I've had to think. It is the first day that Charles will be gone for almost a week. Thank the Lord. A few days ago, Rinee came to me with a fantastic tale that I found hard to believe. In fact, I thought she was making it up to pull me away from Charles. I have known Rinee since I was a child and we grew up together on the plantation. She has been with me since that time and I often find comfort in her company, but she bears such animosity towards Charles. Of course, they don't get along at all and never have.

When she came to me it was on one of those nights that Charles had decided to stay out until the early hours drinking with his friends. She gave me a look that only the devil could have bestowed on her, and I wondered for a long time if indeed the devil hadn't put those awful words into her mouth. But now I know those words to be as true as the rain that falls against my window. She told me that Charles was possessed and that truly he was the devil, for it seems that my Margaret told her daughter of things that Charles does to her and her sister at night when he has had too much whiskey. I didn't believe her and told her that I would have to let her go since the devil had gotten into her.

Then, last night I couldn't sleep for the thoughts that kept rolling around in my head something fierce. I heard Charles stumbling up the stairs and I rose to wait in the shadows. I prayed that he would simply come to bed with me. I willed it. But he did not. Rather he stopped at Rebecca's door, opened it and went in. I saw what the devil has done to my daughters. I feel faint in writing this. Rinee has stayed close by me and I thank You once again, Lord, for her.

My sweet Rebecca is only fourteen years old and

she is with child. From the first, she told me that the boy who does chores for the sisters and Charles got her this way. I believed her and Charles flew into a rage that lasted for days. He nearly beat the child to death. Thankfully, I was able to stop him long enough to turn his hand to myself. I know that if I do not do something soon, Charles will kill my daughter and her baby. She is almost full term and I suspect will deliver most any day. I have longed to talk to Father about this whole sad affair, but I fear that he will stand by Charles. With his power and influence there is nothing that he can not do and will not do to hide this awful truth.

I have spoken with Rinee, the only friend that I have here in this God-forsaken wilderness. She told me she knew of a drifter in town who would be willing to work for supper and he would be very discreet about the work he would be doing for me. Rinee told me that it would be possible to hide Rebecca in the fruit cellar for a spell if this fellow dug it further in and added on a few small rooms. It would be a temporary place to put her until I could get the money to send her to live with my relatives in New York. She said that we could tell Charles that Rebecca died in birthing. Oh Lord, I see no other alternative, no other way. I have no money except for the household fund that has been spent for the month. If there is any other way, please tell me now. Blessed Virgin, tell me now.

Judith Ann Lillian Winslow

Ashley looked sadly away from the window. "So they put her down in the fruit cellar to have her baby." She went and sat on the couch next to Catherine.

"You know, she thought she was being punished for something she had done wrong against God. The poor girl. God only knows how long she was down there in the darkness. In the dream I had, her baby looked to be at least three years old."

Catherine shuddered. "I can't imagine. It seems so cruel, and yet Judith could find no other way to defend her. Here she was stuck, out in the wilderness with a nut for a husband, and no one to turn to except this Rinee.

Ashley shook her head. "I think that they took pretty good care of each other. I think that Judith taught Rinee how to read and write. It seems to me that they were both pretty smart."

Catherine nodded. "It just seems like such a cruel method. I would have taken off and run like hell for the hills."

Ashley held up her hand. "In those days a woman had very little power or say over any part of her life or money. The man was the head of the household. For her to pack up and run would have been suicide. I think that she found the only way out."

"Pretty strong motive to murder her old man, don't you think?"

Ashley frowned. "For which one. Any of them could have done it."

Catherine shook her head. "I was talking about Judith. I think she was the one."

In a panic, Emily stepped back two or three

times. She tripped over someone else's feet and could not regain her balance. She fell backwards, all the while keeping her eye on the presence standing in the doorway. Teri fell on the bed with the remains. Patricia fell on the floor. And Emily fell on Patricia.

The specter stood tall in the doorway. He didn't move. He seemed to fill the entire room with his presence. For a moment, he just stared, the rain dripping down off the brim of his hat. His eyes seemed cold, without even a glimmer of mercy in them. Emily could not find her voice. She simply stared at him and studied him.

The flashlights flickered on some sort of metal pieces he wore on his chest. Then, as quickly as he appeared, he was gone, leaving behind only the residue of cool, foul blackness.

Teri scrambled off of the bed and began tearing off her raincoat. She looked sick to her stomach.

Patricia scrambled up off the floor.

Emily brushed off her skirt and turned calmly to the other women. "Well," she declared, "at least it wasn't as bad as the last time the guy came to our room."

"Let me out of here. I don't care. I want the hell out."

Teri started toward the doorway, but Emily grabbed her so that they were face to face. There would be no argument, Emily saw. Teri was determined to leave.

Emily wrapped her raincoat around Teri's shoulders and said soothingly, "Wait for us outside, okay?"

Teri nodded and without another word left the fruit cellar.

Emily turned to Patricia. She said under her breath, "The other room that Ashley told us about is gone. I wonder if somebody has filled it in or something. Do we dare try to find it, or do you want to give up?"

It took Patricia only a moment of consideration before she said, "Hell no. I'm right behind you."

Emily smiled. "Hopefully not — I still have fingernail marks on my arm from the last time you were right behind me."

Cautiously, they made their way through the short corridor. Wherever the room had been a hundred years ago, there was no sign of it now. Emily pressed her hand against the earthen wall. As soon as she touched it, powerful emotions stirred in her mind and awakened: anger, resentment and the desire for revenge crashed like violent waves at high tide.

"There's something here," she said.

Patricia nodded in agreement. "I think this is a false wall. The room must still exist right on the other side." Patricia tried to gouge the wall. "Damn!" she spat. She'd broken a fingernail.

Emily left and came back about ten minutes later with a little shovel she and Teri found in the gardener's shed. With all her strength, she hit the compacted dirt with the spade end of the shovel. Some of the earth gave way. With the next few blows, more of the dirt crumbled away, exposing another wall built of stone. Upon closer examination, she discovered that the rocks had been haphazardly cemented together. It seemed that whoever did the job did it quickly, heedless of the gaps left behind.

Patricia held her flashlight up to the hole and peered in. "Well," she announced, "there's another one in here."

Emily looked in. This one was dressed in the clothes of a man. It was the same man who had destroyed the room she and Teri occupied. She figured that it was the same man in Ashley's dreams. "Let's try and see if we can tear down the wall a bit more."

Emily pushed on one of the rocks to see if she could dislodge it. As the rock gave way, so did half of the wall. She managed to pull her hand out in time to keep it from being crushed. At the same time, she felt a cold wind suddenly blow through her body in such a rush that she lost control of her senses for a moment.

"You have set him free and now none of you are safe."

Concerned, Emily turned to Patricia. Patricia looked puzzled. "What did you say?"

"I didn't say a word," Patricia said, fear in her eyes.

"I heard you say something," Emily said, feeling her own fear mounting inside her.

"It sounded like me, but I didn't say anything."

Emily turned slightly, and suddenly there appeared before them Judith Ann Lillian Winslow. A rosary hung from her hands. Her face was old and wrinkled.

"It's too late. You have set him free and now he will have the power to gain what he wants." Her blue eyes moved from Emily to Patricia.

Emily moved forward slightly but the woman did not disappear as she'd expected. She was close enough to reach out and touch the old woman. "What does he want?"

"Revenge," she whispered tiredly. She turned and moved through the hallway. The only sound that could be heard was the stiffness of her skirts rustling.

Catherine read silently to herself as Ashley stared out the window. Evening was coming early due to the storm. She could see the flashes of lightning illuminate the horizon. The worst of the storm was not over yet.

Ashley wondered how the others were coming along. They would have to give up their search before long. It would soon be dark. Somewhere in the back of her mind, Ashley knew that they had found the cellar. She gave up hoping that this was all just one bad dream and that she would wake up in her own bed in her apartment.

"Listen to this," Catherine said, breaking the silence. "It's from eighteen ninety-two."

My heart should be overjoyed with the pleasure of knowing that my eldest daughter will be taking the veil at the Convent of Our Lady of Sorrows tomorrow morning in a special ceremony, but I'm alarmed. I'm aware, as my baby sister Agnes has been with the Benedictine sisters for a number of years, that one does not enter the convent and take the veil on the same morning. I'm not aware of this ever happening.

Yet Charles' sister, Mother Mary Agatha, assures me that Father McClaron has gotten special permission from the Pope to do so. All the while I sat with her I could not shake the feeling that I was being lied to. Charles and his sister treat me as though I am ignorant and most times I must admit that I feel this to be true, but I know some things about my church.

The other thing that has troubled me are the bruises on Margaret's face. Her lip was bleeding when Rinee and I came in from the gardening yesterday morning. The bruises came later. I know, but she won't tell me, but I know that Charles had something to do with the beating she so obviously got. She won't tell me why he did it. As far as I knew, he was asleep in our room when Rinee and I left to do the morning chores. Lord knows the animals would starve without Rinee, her daughter Clara, and I. I do believe that this house would have fallen down around our ears by now. Anyhow, later on, Charles demanded to see me in the study as though I was one of the servants in the big house back home. When I came in and sat down he announced that we were going to take a trip to the Convent of Our Lady of Sorrows to see his sister. That is one thing that I had never done in all of the time I have been here. There's an old picture of her, but I have never met the woman.

He and his sister told me then that Margaret would be entering the convent on the morrow. They said that Margaret had come to Mother Mary Agatha and asked to enter the community. This I might have believed, but they said that she would be taking the vows and the veil on the same day. When I opened my mouth to question this, I got a look from Charles

123

that would have killed anyone else dead on the spot. I have not questioned it since.

Last night, Charles came in drunk from one of his many poker games he finds in town. He told me that the devil had gotten into all of our children, Charles Jr. included. He said that Rebecca was lucky that she had died because he just couldn't bear to have to take the burden himself like he had to with Charles Jr. I listened. Now as I sit here and write, my heart is filled with grief once again. I feel as though I am grieving over the death of my son again.

Charles told me that the night Charles Jr. died, he was with him. He said that he had taken Charley into town with him on one of his many excursions where he did God knows what. There was a lot of liquor to be had and everyone got very intoxicated, except Charley. I could see the anger in his eyes as he talked. It seemed to me as though he were reliving it all over again, thousands of miles away. Charley never got along with his father and in fact had gone around a time or two with him in the past. Charles said that his friends and he had found a woman of disdain and had pooled together enough money to buy her for Charley. To make him a man, he said. But Charley would have nothing to do with it at all. After a few choice words, that I dare not repeat, to his father, Charley wanted to leave. Lord, the blood that runs in my veins turns cold with the thought of what Charles must have put the child through. I shudder to imagine that night, when Charles raised his hand to our son, my son, for the last time. Charles beat him until the child didn't move anymore. He was only fourteen. Not even hardly a man.

Lord, I have lost all of my children now. Charley

went to his grave at his own father's hand. Rebecca, Lord, Rebecca is lost to me now. Rinee and I will try to bring her and the baby out of the cellar when I know that Charles will be away for a while. But her mind is not awfully clear anymore. I think that all that has happened to her, and having a child so young, has made her weak of mind. We still have not enough to get her back East where she will be safe with my sister. Perhaps that time has passed forever. And now my Margaret, my sweet Margaret is lost to me too. She will be locked away in that convent and I may never see her again, not even when Charles is away.

I saw how his sister looked at me yesterday. I know that he has convinced her as well as the rest of the town that I am the reason for our hardships. Lord, sometimes I cannot help but believe that I am. I beg of you, my Sweet Blessed Mary, to pray for us. To pray for all of us, now and at the hour of our death.

Judith Ann Lillian Winslow

Catherine pinched her brows together and laid the book down next to her. She thought about the entry she'd just read. It was indeed strange. Never had she heard of such a case where the Pope allowed a woman to enter a convent and take the veil on the same day. It hadn't been that way for centuries, and certainly not in the last hundred or so years. She wondered what kind of a community this was. She had heard of strange orders that had sprung up in the past, and of course there had been many schisms through the years — whole countries had parted from the church — but it would be highly unusual that this was one such order. Still, that could be the only explanation for a girl entering the convent and take the veil the same day.

She thought about the years she had spent in the convent in Chicago. In the beginning, she had been thrilled to know that she alone was called by God to do service for Him in the world. She cruised through her postulancy and novitiate without much problem. She owned the zest to make it through.

Some days were very hard, especially when she missed her family and friends back in Portland, but through prayer she made it through the homesickness that plagued her. She poured her mind and heart into the service she was called to do, and began to memorize some of the very long offices that were said in the morning. Engraved in her memory were the Stations of the Cross and more. She loved the Benediction the best. She could kneel for hours before the exposed sacrament and pray, much as she envisioned the saints had done before her.

Slowly, she learned to let go of worldly things and concentrate on those of the soul. Not only of her soul but the souls of all people. She learned to obey the Rule of her community — not break the silence in the mornings, how to abstain from those foods that appealed to her the most, and to humbly eat those things which she found she liked the least.

She knew about the "particular friendships" that seemed to form around her, though some were never spoken of. She knew that sisters were having affairs against the vows that they had taken. Some of the affairs had lasted for many years. She was indifferent to the gossip — it wasn't her concern — until she was sent out to teach for the first time away from the motherhouse.

It was a small convent nestled in one of the larger suburbs that flanked Chicago. The convent was actually an old mansion converted to house twenty sisters. She, as Sister Catherine, was the twentieth nun to fill the house. The nuns were to teach at a private, Catholic girls' school.

Catherine was filled with excitement at the prospects of putting all of her learning into teaching. To her mind, nothing could go wrong.

That was when the visions began. She could see things and predict things sometimes months ahead. Sometimes she could touch the belongings of another sister and know her deepest secrets. In fear, she kept them to herself until she couldn't bear it any longer.

One evening, she went to the head sister. Once she opened her mouth she could not stop talking about her visions until she realized that she had gone too far to turn back. Catherine half expected to be drummed out of the convent for being possessed by the devil, but Sister Felicity surprised her with her understanding. For half the night, they talked about psychic phenomena. Catherine came away convinced that she was like many other people in the world and that she was not possessed by some evil spirit. Sister Felicity encouraged Catherine to come to her any time. She would be glad to listen.

Somewhere in the back of Catherine's mind a bell sounded, but she longed for the friendship that she found in the other nun. It was not long before the other nuns were talking about her and Felicity. It was the first time that she had ever heard her name associated with the term "particular friendship."

Worried, she went to Felicity about the rumors, hoping that she'd would put a stop to them. At first Felicity said nothing. And then, very slowly, she began to tell Catherine about the deep feelings she had for her. Catherine was appalled. All she could think of was her vows. Looking back on it now, she knew that she had had feelings for the woman, but she had failed to name them.

Catherine began to avoid Sister Felicity at all costs. Her actions hurt and angered Felicity to the point that she phoned the Mother Superior at the motherhouse and talked about Catherine for almost an hour. Before Catherine knew what was happening, she was moved back to the motherhouse. She was called into the Mother Superior's office and lectured on the sins of the flesh, her vows to the church and the Lord, and on the powers that the devil sometimes gave to some people to pull them away from God. The last words her Mother Superior said were, "Be sure where your soul rests, Sister. This community will not tolerate any more of your so-called predictions."

Even in doing penance and assigning herself the dirtiest tasks in the convent, Catherine couldn't stop the visions from haunting her. The last one that she had was of Mother Superior. In her mind, she saw the snow falling so hard that the lights of the railroad were not visible until the car was right on top of them. She saw the twisted metal of the car. She heard the train wheels squeal to a stop — much too late. She saw the bodies of the other nuns lying in pools of blood on the seats. She saw Mother Superior dead in the back seat.

For a whole day she fought with herself not to tell anyone. Then, through prayer, she knew what she must do. After the evening vespers, Catherine set up a time to see the Mother Superior. As tactfully as she could, she told her of the imminent accident she had seen, and she begged her not to go to the conference the following night. She could still see the anger on the woman's face as she ordered Catherine out of her office.

The following evening, all four of the nuns were killed, just as Catherine had said they would be. A week later, Catherine was asked to leave the convent. Torn by what she had felt was the right thing to do and by what her church taught her was right, she left with a bitter ache in her gut. Until now, she had never looked back.

Ashley broke into her thoughts. "So what are you thinking?"

Catherine smiled. "I was just remembering. You know, there's something that doesn't sound right with what they told Judith. First of all, a woman can't take the veil on the same day she enters and second of all, I think I know why Daddy might have sent Margaret to the convent. Listen, I saw Margaret and Clara saying their good-byes the other day in my room, and they were more than friends."

A smile crossed Ashley's lips. "You've got to be kidding me. I didn't think there was any such thing as lesbians back then."

Catherine laughed. "My dear, there have been gay people since the world began."

"So Daddy puts Margaret into the convent with

his beloved sister to watch over his evil offspring, huh?" Ashley jumped up and began to pace.

Catherine smiled to herself. All it took was to get Ashley away from her own problems and onto someone else's. She could practically see the thoughts whirling in Ashley's mind.

* * * * *

Emily, Patricia and Teri filed into the house calling up from the hallway for Catherine and Ashley to join them. Emily pulled off her coat. The three of them were soaked to the skin, and the rain still pelted against the house.

Emily refused to change out of her clothes wanting to tell everybody about the discovery of the fruit cellar and of what they found inside. By the time she finished, she was almost breathless.

Teri shoved a hot cup of coffee in front of her and gave one to Patricia as well, then settled in next to Emily at the table.

"Who do you think it is, Judith or Rebecca?" Ashley asked as she pulled up a seat next to Catherine.

Patricia shrugged. "I have a feeling that it was that poor child they shoved down there."

Emily agreed. "I think that it was Rebecca. And there was no question about who the other person was."

Ashley traced the rim of her cup. "So whoever killed the old man shoved him down in the cellar and slapped up a wall to hide him."

"So, with the old man dead, why did they leave Rebecca down there to die? It doesn't make any sense." Catherine took a sip from her cup.

Patricia offered, "Perhaps she had just gotten so used to living down there that she stayed even after her father died."

For a while no one else said anything, then Ashley asked, "Teri, didn't you say that the family disappeared one night without a word to anyone? When was that, do you know?"

Teri nodded slowly, her brow furrowed in thought. "That particular piece of gossip went from generation to generation because it was so odd. The entire family just picked up and left. The convent burned down around that time as well."

"Well, the way I see it," Catherine said, standing, "we have to answer a few more questions before we'll be allowed to leave here. One, who killed Charles Winslow? Two, who killed Sister Mary Margaret? And three, why would this particular family haunt a whole line of women in Ashley's family? I think that it's rather obvious that there's some sort of connection here."

Emily snapped her fingers. She had a thought. "Pat, do you have any family on your side that might have lived here back then?"

"No, my side of the family is from New Jersey. As far as I know, we've always lived there. Marshal's family came from Europe. We moved to Oregon because of his job. What is it you're driving at?"

Emily took a moment before she answered. She felt something coming — it was like hearing a voice from very far away. She shrugged. "I thought maybe your family could've had a feud or something with this family, and, well you know, perhaps someone on your side did in Charles."

Patricia pursed her lips together and tapped her

forefinger against them. "I see. No, as far as I know my side's always lived in New Jersey. Always."

Emily shook her head, hoping that the voice would come closer to her. She squeezed her eyes shut, then blinked. "I feel as though I'm in the right forest but barking up the wrong tree."

Ashley looked astonished. "What you're saying is that Charles Winslow's blood is on our hands? Mine and my Mother's?"

Emily paused, looking into Ashley's eyes. "Yes," she said simply.

CHAPTER TWELVE

One by one, they shuffled tiredly off to bed, leaving Catherine, who was reading the journal, and Ashley, who sat in the silence thinking.

Not all Catherine's attention was devoted to the journal. She was concerned about Ashley. From the strain on her face, Catherine could tell that Ashley was fighting sleep. The old fears had apparently come back to her. She closed the journal as she chose her words carefully.

"Ashley, why don't you go on up to bed? You look so tired."

Ashley shook her head. "I can't. I can't go up there again and dream that same nightmare all over again. It was so real. I could feel everything that she felt all of those years ago."

Catherine understood. "Listen, would it help if I came up with you and stayed until you fell asleep?"

Ashley shook her head again. "You don't understand. I'm afraid of going to sleep. I'm afraid of dreaming. Besides, I couldn't ask you to do that." She vacated the chair she had been sitting in for the last two hours and stared out the window at the retreating storm. It had raged for hours, but Catherine had to wonder if it was only the eye of the storm passing through and the worst was yet to come.

Ashley started when she realized that Catherine was standing behind her.

"I know that it's been hard for you to be here with me. I know how you feel about me." Catherine sighed. "I wish I could change things, but I can't. It would be wrong."

Ashley turned to face her. "Wrong for who, Cathy? You, your fiancé, me, your church? I love you, and no matter who you are, no matter what you do, no matter where you go, you can't change the way I feel for you. It just is." Her words were fraught with conviction, and there were tears welling in her eyes. She turned, and without a word, left the parlor.

Lost in her own thoughts, Catherine stared out the window. She couldn't deny the feelings that she had tried to suppress. Yet she knew what the teachings of her religion were. She was engaged to be married. She felt as though she were being torn apart. Should she follow her heart or her mind? She knew that she would have to make a decision soon — before she had no choices left.

Ashley found herself in the study. She scanned the bookshelves. One of the volumes caught her eye and she pulled it off of the shelf. The pages were yellowed from age and dust coated the binding.

She sat down at the desk and opened the book. There were many pages filled with pictures of horrible-looking demonic creatures in all sorts of scenes. A book on demonology in the library of a man whose sister was a Mother Superior at a convent just down the road? That was a surprise. She glanced up at the bookshelf again. Slowly, she read the other titles near the one she had pulled out. All of the topics dealt with different phases of the supernatural, from mysticism to hauntings.

It seemed odd to Ashley that a man such as Charles Winslow would have any interest in the occult. "Unless," she said aloud, "he was seeking something beyond the reach of the flesh." Her words shocked her. She could hear the tension and the strain of exhaustion in them. Inside, she knew that she could not run from sleep for much longer.

Ashley pushed the thoughts away and chose another book from the shelf. It was a subject that suited her suspicions. The topic was immortality.

Ashley wasn't sure when she had fallen asleep, but she woke with a start. Through her foggy mind, she scanned the room. The study was filled with the flickering illumination of kerosene lamps. She knew she was dreaming.

The man that she recognized as Charles Winslow retrieved the book titled *Immortality* from the shelf. He crossed the study to his desk and sat with his fingers pressing against his lips. His cold blue eyes stared at the closed book for quite a while, though none of his thoughts crossed the rugged face of the man.

Finally, he opened the book slowly and turned the first hundred or so pages of the immense tome. The core of the book had been carefully carved out, revealing a wonderful hiding place for private things, things that he wanted no one else to see, things that would condemn him in a court of law.

He had just returned from one of his many trips to Portland. There he consulted with a secret society of men with whom he shared the same interests. None of the five men came from Portland and in fact, Charles was the only one who lived within a hundred-mile radius of the city.

Not for a single moment did it come to the men that their group, their leader, or their actions were immoral. With hungry eyes focused on something just beyond their reach, just beyond their wealth and fame, they gathered to do what would have repelled other men. They had one aim, one precious golden egg promised to them, these "special" men. Immortality.

Charles savored the word. It was the one thing that he could not buy, could not steal, and it was the one thing he longed for. To live forever. He knew that it wouldn't be long now. The leader had promised each of them a piece of that which they struggled for. Briefly, he mulled over the events of the last meeting.

They had gathered secretly, as usual, and drank together until the sun beamed through the windows of the dingy hotel room. It was then that the special envoy from their leader revealed to them where they were to gather that night. They had met there once or twice before. It was a place that Charles was assigned to find when he was told by the leader to move to Astoria.

That night, the men gathered, five miles from Portland in the cave carved by nature out of the side of a mountain. There was no chance of the police ever finding the spot. Only the men in the group knew where it was, and they knew that the punishment of turning against the group went much further than just death.

The cave was lit with torches that ran deep into the throat of the cavern. Charles walked with the others calmly through the winding tunnel. As they approached the wide den where the tunnel ended, they saw that the envoy himself was already there. He was dressed in a robe similar to the others, differing in color only. Whereas the others wore black robes, the delegate wore red.

There were no words of greeting, no exchanges of niceties and no handshakes. That had all been taken care of yesterday. Tonight the meeting had one purpose — business.

On a slab of rugged stone, a young, attractive woman lay tied up and gagged. Charles knew she was the same courtesan Charles had enjoyed the pleasure of the night before. He enjoyed the feeling of excitement that ran warmly through his blood. She had pleased him immensely several times the previous night, but he knew that his greatest pleasure was to come.

The men gathered in their specified spots around the slab. In low, rhythmic tones they began to chant. Very slowly at first. Very low at first. The woman gazed at them fearfully.

The woman was about to speak when she felt the sudden and forceful pressure applied to her chest. A warm liquid spread down her belly and across her chest. From the single wound in her chest blood gushed.

With sadistic glee, Charles watched the changes of expression on her face. First panic, then shock, and then absolution — all wiped away by the mask of death. His hair stood up on his arms with goosebumps of pleasure. Silently, he took the cup that was offered to him and sipped from it. Then he took the bloody stiletto and approached the corpse that lay so still on the cold slab. Smiling, he cut the pinky finger from her left hand.

Ashley watched as Charles dug in the pocket of his vest. From it, he pulled a small, white object and inspected it as though it was a valuable jewel. She realized that it was the tip of a finger. Desperately, she fought to wake as she was forced to watch the grizzly scene.

Charles dropped his treasure in the hole of the tome. He had four other bones in the cache. His mind whirled. The first four were strangers, the last two must be family. These two he was left to do on his own. Then he knew he would achieve the coveted position. A position that the leader had already achieved. A position he wanted.

He plotted his next moves carefully. He had already chosen the two he wanted. Both would be easy because they lived in the same place. In his own way, he had wheedled out of his sister the information he needed. He now knew where Margaret and his sister slept. The rest, he knew, would be nearly effortless.

With his mind made up, he removed the stiletto from one of the drawers in the desk. He pushed it into a sheath, secured it to his belt, then went to the door.

A storm raged and Charles found himself fighting wind and biting sheets of rain. He couldn't see the convent as he followed the muddy trail through the forest. With the aid of a flash of lightning, Charles saw a figure moving on the trail just a few yards ahead of him. He knew in an instant who it was.

He chose to follow Clara, suddenly overcome with curiosity and anger. This could only serve to dampen his plans. He watched in the momentary flashes of lightning as Clara made her way slowly to the far side of the convent. Finally, she stopped underneath a cluster of trees. Charles watched her struggle to light a kerosene lamp. When the wind calmed for a moment, she quickly turned the flame up as high as it would go, then turned it down. She did this several times in the lull of the wind.

Charles knew that she was signaling for Margaret. Without thinking, he moved closer to the wall. His chances of getting to Clara without her seeing him coming were slim, due to the flashes of lightning. In his fury, he turned and followed the wall around the to the other side of the convent. There would always be time to get rid of Clara later.

As he walked against the wind and rain, jealousy fed his anger. In addition, his plans had been foiled. When he came around the last wall and saw Margaret standing there near the cliff, throwing her shoes into the water, he could feel nothing but rage burning inside of him. He ran with his teeth clenched, hoping that the lightning would not betray his presence. With satisfaction growing in him, he watched as Margaret plummeted to her death on the rocks below.

Catherine sat with the journal after Ashley left and tried to bury her feelings in Judith's story. She had only a scant few pages to go. She could almost predict the final entry in the journal, but she knew that none of the final pages would make sense without reading the pages that preceded them.

Soon, Catherine nodded off and the journal fell from her hands. The clock had just struck one o'clock in the morning. The house was still.

Gretchen awoke in the silence of the small world she had been forced to live in. She couldn't remember who she was, or how she had come to be there. When she probed her mind, she found only pain. The pit of her stomach ached dully.

It wasn't until she saw the light of the lamp did she prop herself weakly on one elbow to see who was coming. Vaguely, she knew she should be afraid. A memory warned her that danger was coming. She hadn't the energy or the will to fight any longer.

As the lamp drew closer to her, she saw part of the face of a woman. A white cloth encased most of her head. She smiled gently. For a moment, Gretchen thought that she was an angel coming to take her away from the room.

"Are you my guardian angel?"

The woman laughed softly. "I am your friend. I'll help you soon."

Gretchen watched her disappear. She knew that it was just a dream, like the dream of her mother standing outside in the rain. She fell back into a deep sleep.

Emily woke from sleep as though something had shaken her awake. At last, she thought. She gently shook Teri awake.

"What," Teri mumbled in her sleep.

"I got it!" Emily said triumphantly as she sprang from the bed.

Teri stirred and opened her eyes. "What's going on?"

Emily threw on her clothes hastily.

"Emily, it's almost two in the morning, can't it wait until tomorrow?" Teri asked, pushing off the covers.

Emily shook her head. "I know the relationship between the Windlows and the Winslows. They're one and the same. It's so obvious. Just take away an *s* and add a *d*. Simple, that's why Ashley's been haunted by the dreams and why it's gone on for several generations. It's because Ashley and Pat are related to the Winslows by blood."

Teri hastily dressed as Emily explained.

Emily reached for the door and found she was unable to turn the knob. The door was locked from the outside. Suddenly, her mind flashed on Ashley. She was in trouble. This time, as always, Ashley reached out to her with her mind. She could feel the other's panic and fear. Emily knew it could be only a matter of minutes before it was too late.

Patricia woke to the sound of muffled voices and pounding. At first she wasn't sure where the sounds were coming from. She listened in the darkness of her room. It seemed to be coming from the room down the hall. The room Emily and Teri occupied.

She sprang from her bed and searched for the travel flashlight. Finding it, she made her way across the room only to find that someone had locked her door.

With her ear pressed to the keyhole, Patricia listened as shouts rang down the hall. She caught most of it. Emily and Teri were locked in their room as well, and Ashley was in some sort of trouble.

With this, Patricia shook the doorknob, hoping to dislodge it enough to slip the old lock. After a few moments of struggling, she found her labors to be fruitless. She bent down and peered through the keyhole.

Catherine woke to the sounds of knocking. When she opened her eyes she discovered that she had slept the night away in the chair in the parlor. She moved lazily out of the chair and stretched her cramped muscles. Glancing around, she wondered where the journal had gone. It seemed to have disappeared .

The knocking sounded more insistent the second time. As she moved to the front door, she wondered where everyone was. Suddenly, the door to the kitchen flew open and an old black woman stepped out. She nearly brushed her as she went by.

Confused, Catherine watched the woman open the door. About the time that the two men stepped inside with hats in their hands, Catherine knew that she was dreaming and the woman who she watched was Rinee.

She glanced out the window and saw that it was much later than she had first thought it was. The sun was slowly setting. It was late afternoon.

Rinee looked from one haggard face to the other. The expression on her face said that she already knew why the men were here.

Quickly, she hurried to get Judith from the fruit cellar where Rebecca and the child were hidden.

When Judith came to the door, she asked politely, "What is it, Mr. Hannibee?"

The older gentleman worried his hat in his hands

as he tried to find the words to tell the unfortunate woman that her daughter was dead. He found the best way was just to tell her flat out.

Rinee stood behind the woman she had served for all her life and waited. At first, Judith said nothing, then she thanked the men and saw them to the door.

"Margaret was dead," they'd told her, and worse, they believed it was suicide.

Judith's knees gave way under her and she reached for Rinee's arm for support. Rinee led Judith into the parlor and sat next to her on the settee.

Catherine followed them, not by choice, but because she felt something forcing her to move. She could sense their thoughts as she listened to their conversation.

Judith sobbed and allowed Rinee to hold her. She mumbled over and over again. "It's my fault. I killed her. God forgive me, it's my fault."

"Shhh, now baby, shhh, now. God knows it's not your fault." Rinee tried to comfort the woman in her arms much like she had comforted her daughter hours before. She knew that it would come to this. The deaths had to come to an end eventually, and she suspected that Judith was walking very close to the edge of her own sanity.

"Oh, Rinee, she took her own life. How could this have happened?" Judith asked, though she knew the answer was harbored inside of her. She had thought that things would get better if Margaret left. She had thought that things would get better when Rebecca left, but it was all a deception much like the façade that Charles wore when he had come to court her those many years ago. She felt as though she was an old, worn out bridge that just couldn't bear the weight any longer.

"Now, now, you know in your heart that sweet child couldn't have done something like that," Rinee said, sweeping back the woman's hair from her forehead.

"Then what in the world was she doing out there in that horrible storm last night?" Judith wiped her eyes with a handkerchief and looked into the other woman's eyes. It came to her then as she saw the answer reflected back at her. "It can't be true!" She sobbed. "Then my daughter was lost to me anyway."

"I don't believe that my daughter is lost to me. There are so many other bad things in the world that the Lord needs to tend to that I think He had very little time to worry about those who love each other the way that Clara and Miss Margaret loved."

Judith weighed Rinee's words. Considering the evils that lived in the house, it was the lesser of all of them, but she knew in her heart that she would always pray for her daughter's soul.

Rinee sighed as though the entire weight of the world was on her shoulders. She loved Miss Margaret, and in the light of her death she mourned deep within her soul. Later on, she would have time to read from her Bible and pray. For now, however, she had a greater burden to bear.

Judith sensed that Rinee was hiding something from her about the death of her daughter. She could almost hear her thoughts. "Why do you think Margaret was murdered?" she asked.

Rinee was not shocked. There had been many times that Judith had heard her thoughts as they passed through her mind. They had been able to do this since the time that they were both young,and it came as almost second nature to both women.

"Clara saw who killed your daughter, Miss Judith. It was the mister who did it. Clara came to me in the middle of the night last night. She was weeping so, I could hardly make out a word until this morning. She told me that he looked like the devil as he came out of the night the way he did."

Judith held up her hand and stood on shaky knees. For a long moment she said nothing. Rinee feared that Judith had lost control of her mind, for her face suddenly slackened. She rose to her feet and waited for Judith to speak.

Catherine watched with tears in her eyes. She couldn't believe what she had heard, nor could she suppress the grief that Judith was feeling inside of her. Catherine was reading her thoughts as they began to twist and turn. She knew that Judith was nearing insanity. She had lost everything at the hands of the man known as Charles Winslow.

Judith straightened her skirts and faced Rinee with a determined look. "When Charles comes in I'll deal with him. Until then, fetch Rebecca and the child and bring them up to the house. I'll need to tell her about her sister." Rinee turned to leave when she heard Judith say, "I reckon we'll need to pack everything that's of value and put it on the buckboard before Charles comes home. I know the combination to the safe in the study, even though he never knew that I knew." She laughed to herself. "I'll get the money out of there when we're ready to leave after he gets home."

Catherine couldn't define the look of Judith's face.

146

At best she thought that Judith had been pushed over the edge.

Whoever locked Patricia in her bedroom had left the key in the door. She pulled a hanger out of the closet and bent it to fit into the keyhole. She was surprised when she heard the heavy key thump on the floor just on the other side of the door. Carefully, she pushed the hanger under the door and felt blindly for the key. Nothing. She tried again.

She could still hear Emily shouting down the hall and banging her shoulder against the door. Patricia figured that the two could bang on the door all day until their shoulders were sore and the ancient locks would probably not give.

One more time, she thought as she bent the hanger again and shoved it under the door. The second try failed too. Patricia lay face-down on the floor and peered under the door. The only thing that she had succeeded in doing was to push the key farther away from the reach of her hanger. Damn, she thought as she studied the hanger.

Ashley sat in the chair in the study. Her body was relaxed as her head rested on her chest. Her skin was as pale as snow. In her mind she was about to relive the last day of Charles Winslow's life.

* * * * *

The day following Sister Mary Margaret's death, Charles sat in a makeshift tavern with fishermen and locals, drinking and gambling. In the back of his mind he could hear his own fury as it cursed at him for failing to do what he had set out to do the night before. Now he would have to use Judith in place of Margaret. He had hoped to avoid this, not because he loved his wife, but because she filled a spot in his life, and like a comfortable chair, it was hard to get rid of her. He shrugged this off with the thought that even a chair was replaceable.

He had left a message for his sister to expect him after sundown. His hate swelled in his gut at the memory of her sly smile. She'd expect the usual, he knew, just like always. From the time that he was a boy, certain things were understood between them, and this was just one of those things. He felt relief when she had entered the convent those many years ago, but things changed very little. She constantly reminded him that she was the one who raised him when their father had died, leaving them nothing but half a loaf of bread. And it was she who taught him how to manipulate people and things to gain not only what was needed, but what was wanted. How could he deny her one simple thing in the light of all of the sacrifices that she had given for him?

Charles yawned and pulled a pocket watch from his vest. It was time. He threw down his hand of playing cards face up, showing he had nothing more than a pair of threes, scooped his money up off the table and didn't bother to excuse himself. None of the men complained about his leaving, for they feared him.

On horseback, Charles made his way along the

road to the convent. The sun was barely setting and the time he had before dark gave him the opportunity to clear his head. He would have to be swift and quiet to do what had to be done.

With the aid of a full kerosene lamp, Charles located the unused and not well known catacomb entrance to the convent. He hated coming in this way. It reminded him of the closeness of death to all mortal things. Death scared him. It was the only thing that really scared him. Quickly, he made his way through the tombs and climbed the stairs to the chapel.

His sister was waiting there with a lamp next to her on the pew. He found it sick and ironic to see her deep in prayer as she knelt before the great crucifix. Clearing his throat, he distracted her attention from the holy things. She saw him and smiled.

As she came to where he stood near the sacristy behind the altar, Charles could feel his heart flutter with the rush of excitement for what he was about to do. He balled up his fist as she approached him. In the only act of mercy Charles had ever performed in his life, he aimed his punch at her throat, crushing her larynx. Within moments, she lay dead at his feet.

With a great heave, Charles lifted the heavy body to the altar. He had planned to make a sacrifice of his own, but a pang of fear shot through him. All he really needed was the first joint of his sister's pinky finger.

With his grizzly act complete, Charles poured some of the kerosene on the body, more down the center aisle of the chapel, and some on the walls. When the lamp emptied, he took one more look at his dead sister. Emotionless, he threw the lit lamp she had carried to the floor and watched as the floor, pews, and altar caught the spreading flame.

Judith could smell the pungent odor of kerosene on her husband as he came through the door shortly after dusk. Rebecca was somewhere in the house helping Rinee pack up some clothes and other things that they would need.

Judith reflected for a moment on her daughter. She was so much like a child, even though she had grown into a young woman. The stay in the fruit cellar had made her ignorant of the world outside. The thought of what Judith herself had done made icicles run through her blood. She hated what she had become and she wondered if the brunt of her sins that her children had borne could ever be corrected somehow.

Rebecca had reacted much like a child to the death of her sister. She couldn't comprehend that Margaret was gone forever. Heaven wasn't a concept she understood. Judith wondered if she would ever be made to understand the world after all her years of exile. She hoped that somehow when they were as far away from the house as they could get, she could teach her daughter all of the things that a woman should know in order for her to survive.

Judith shook the thoughts out of her mind and inhaled slowly. What she was about to do scared her worse than the fires of hell. The anger that had been suppressed for so many years prodded her on. She went to Charles's study.

What happened next took her by surprise. As she was reaching for the door, an arm reached behind her and grabbed her by the waist. She felt a hand covering her mouth and her nose. In desperation, she struggled to free herself. After a moment, her mind began to fade to black as her body weakened from the lack of oxygen. She fainted.

With wide eyes, the child watched from behind the heavy curtains at the window as a man she didn't know lay her grandmother on the leather chaise. From the desk drawer, he withdrew a small pointed knife. The child dared not breathe, for she feared the man. She could see the evil that surrounded him like a shroud of blackness.

The child cringed as the man raised the knife above his head and plunged it into her grandmother's chest. A tiny sound came from Judith's mouth, followed by silence. She did not stir.

With great satisfaction, Charles backed away from his wife and looked at the stiletto in his hand. He felt no grief, no anger, no pain. He felt blank.

Puzzled, he sat in his chair behind the desk and thought. He ran his hand through his beard. He opened the book on immortality and glanced at the bones inside. He began to feel some anger and as he fed it, he could feel it grow inside of his gut.

When the door suddenly flew open, he thought it was Rinee. It startled him — he hadn't expected such an interruption with his dead wife on the couch.

"What is the meaning of this," he said, raising his voice in anger.

"Margaret's dead," the voice said from the doorway. He couldn't see who was standing there but the voice seemed familiar.

"What in God's name are you talking about?" He squinted to see who had invaded his domain.

The voice simply repeated, "Margaret's dead."

Charles started to rise from his chair when he heard the sounds of skirts rustling and Rebecca stepped out of the shadows of the doorway. She fired one shot that struck him in the forehead. The last thought that passed through his mind was one of remorse. He had not completed his mission, and as always, the thing that he coveted the most slipped from his grasp.

Ashley's eyes snapped open. Her body became rigid for a moment and then relaxed. Blackness. Nothingness. Then a light, not from a kerosene lamp, but from an electric bulb in a lamp near the desk. The laughter that came from her didn't belong to Ashley and she realized that Charles Winslow must have found a way to take control of her mind, her consciousness. She could feel him within her. She could hear his thoughts as clearly as if they were her own. She tried to fight but found that all her strength had left her. She surrendered.

Catherine woke to the sound of thunder. She jumped up from her chair and the journal dropped to the floor. Bewildered, she stood in the middle of the parlor. Again the thunder cracked the sky and shook the house. Must be one hell of a storm, Catherine thought as she peered out the window into the darkness. A flash of lightning lit the sky all the way to the horizon line.

Catherine stumbled out of the parlor, only to discover the front door standing wide open. The wind banged it against the wall, making a din that seemed to echo through the house. As she closed the door against the elements, Catherine heard a laughter that pealed through the house. It was the most chilling sound she had ever heard. For a moment, she thought that it was the devil, then reminded herself of the impossibilities. She shivered.

Patricia managed to hook the key and was attempting to pull it through the crack beneath the door when she heard the laughter. It raised the hair on the back of her neck. With renewed fear, she hastily pulled the key into the room. She could no longer hear Emily and Teri beating on the door. They'd probably heard the laughter too, Patricia thought. Her stomach was twisting in knots. She didn't want to believe that her daughter might be dead, but she couldn't fight the feeling that she had succumbed.

Emily felt a chill run through her body. She felt Ashley release her hold on life. A scream welled up in her throat and exploded from her mouth. "Ashley!"

* * * * *

Catherine followed the sound of laughter to the closed study door. She felt suddenly very cold. Without hesitation she flung the door open with a bang against the wall. She saw Ashley. Her face was covered with perspiration. Catherine took a few steps into the room and froze. Ashley held a small knife in her right hand that was poised over her left hand.

"Get out," Ashley said, her voice thin and straining.

Catherine moved closer to the desk. She could see the wispy face of another superimposed across Ashley's face. It was Charles Winslow. "Ashley, my God."

Another voice, not her own, boomed. "If you don't surrender to me, I'll kill her. I'll kill everything you love."

Catherine saw a flash of familiarity cross Ashley's face. Pleading eyes looked at her. "Get out, Catherine."

"Fight him, Ashley." Catherine didn't move from her spot. She sensed Ashley growing weaker as the spirit once again overpowered her.

"Surrender to me, you whore." Ashley spewed the words of Charles Winslow. Suddenly, her body went limp and she slumped over the desk. Catherine waited to see who had won the fight. Her greatest fears were answered when Ashley stood. Her face was twisted with a cruel grin.

"Ashley, damn you, fight him. Fight," Catherine pleaded, looking around the room. She knew that Ashley was somewhere very close. "I love you, Ashley. Fight him."

* * * * *

Ashley heard a voice next to her. It was very close. It said, "Charles." Ashley felt herself turn to the voice. There, standing in the middle of the room, was Judith. The worried lines of age were gone from her face. She looked younger and stronger. At her side was Margaret and Rebecca.

"Release her." Judith moved forward slightly to confront the man.

"You don't command me, woman." Charles turned his attention back to gaining the prize he had worked for. With this last treasure he would win what he had been promised a hundred years ago.

"Charles, you fool. The group leader lied to you. You have gained nothing with your cruelty, with your killing, other than the eternal damnation of hell. It's time to rest. Someone knows what happened here. The truth shall be your memorial and all will remember you as the cruel murderer that you were. This shall be the only immortality you will ever receive."

"You are a lying bitch. I have the power to destroy you forever. I killed you once and I shall kill you again."

Judith moved closer to Ashley and she peered into the eyes of her demented husband. "Release her."

"I . . . " The voice coming from Ashley's mouth faltered. Catherine could see the struggle going on from within, as the two souls fought for the right of possession. "I'll see you in hell before I'll release her."

The hand that held the knife slashed the air and Catherine jumped to avoid the blade. Charles could feel his grasp on the woman fading and he struggled to hold on.

Ashley could feel Charles releasing control of her body. She crumbled to the floor and fell into blackness.

Catherine heard Charles scream as a force she couldn't explain entered the room, swept through it and then dissipated. While the force occupied the room she couldn't move. It was as if her muscles were made of concrete. For the first time since she entered the house, Catherine couldn't feel the presence of what she would later describe as amorality. She went to Ashley's side. She looked dead. Through her tears she felt for any signs of life but found none.

Patricia unlocked the door and raced down the hall. She stopped only long enough to unlock the other door and disappeared down the stairs two at a time. Emily and Teri followed close behind.

Emily found Catherine and Ashley exactly as she had envisioned them.

"Ashley," she screamed.

Teri took Patricia into her arms and guided her out of the room. She was almost in hysterics, blaming herself and the house for her daughter's demise.

As Ashley found her way out of the darkness, she

saw the face of Sister Mary Margaret looking down at her. She felt no pain, no anguish, no tribulation.

The nun smiled and reached for Ashley. "Come," she said, leading the way. "There's something yet that needs to be cared for here."

Ashley followed without questioning.

Instantly, Ashley found herself in one of the rooms she and Catherine had looked through on the third floor. There was a trap door they hadn't noticed before in the huge walk-in closet and it was hanging open. Ashley could hear someone shuffling around in the darkness. After a moment, a ladder come slowly down to the floor and a pair of legs appeared.

Ashley waited to see who the intruder was. Slowly the legs became a body and then a face. Ashley recoiled. In the man's arms was the child she had seen in her vision. It was Gretchen. The child lolled unconsciously in the man's arms. The nun looked pleadingly at Ashley, then vanished.

In a flash, Ashley found herself in the study. On the floor was her own body lying in Catherine's arms. Catherine was weeping, and Ashley longed to comfort her. She could feel no pain.

"Ashley." A voice came from behind her.

"Poppa," Ashley said excitedly. She ran into his arms. Marshal smiled and allowed himself a moment to feel the child in his arms. When he stepped back, his face was marred with serious concern. "You have to go back. It's not your time."

Ashley shook her head, but she knew that it was in vain. Already she could feel herself being pulled back into her body.

Ashley felt a rush. She was back inside her body again. Her finger throbbed with pain. She thought it was the sweetest thing in the world. Slowly she opened her eyes. As her vision cleared, she saw the weeping faces of Catherine and Emily before her. She smiled.

"Oh my God, Ashley," Catherine said, embracing her. "You scared the hell out of us."

Ashley struggled to find her voice. She remembered what Sister Mary Margaret had shown her. It would only be a matter of seconds before the child disappeared from the house forever. She grabbed Emily by the collar. "Listen to me. Gretchen's in the house. Upstairs. Third floor. There's someone with her. You have to stop him. She's almost dead."

Emily sprang to her feet and motioned for Teri to join her. They bolted out of the study just in time to see the figure of a man hurrying toward the entranceway.

In an act of desperation, Emily grabbed the fireplace shovel and hit him on the back of the head. Gretchen dropped from his arms and, stunned, he turned toward Emily.

Teri gasped. "Randy Taylor, you son of a bitch."

Blood trickled down the back of Taylor's head and stained his white T-shirt. Gingerly, he touched the wound and pulled his hand away. "You cut me. You bitch."

"I'll give you more than that if you come near any of us," Emily shouted, brandishing the shovel.

"What in the hell do you think you're doing?" Teri asked, aghast.

Taylor shrugged, a smug smile playing on his lips. "She's my kid too, and I have the right to do with her what I want. I'm the father." He took a step forward, ignoring Emily.

"You're talking about her as though she were a possession. She's a child, for the love of God. Why? Why would you do this? If your intentions were to hurt me, you already did that a long time ago." Anger flashed in Teri's eyes as the thunder rolled outside the house.

Taylor grabbed the shovel and ripped it out of Emily's hands. He threw the it down the hallway. "I'm taking the kid, understand?" He waved his finger in front of Teri's face.

"I don't think so, son," a voice said from behind him. "I think we'll wait for the sheriff and the ambulance." Agnes Dupree stepped into the room. There was a gun in her hand.

Taylor froze. "Come on now, Agnes. You're the one who told me about Teri living with all sorts of trash and messing around with other women. You said it yourself that she was living in sin, or have you forgotten? I was just doing it to get her away from this ... this dyke."

"You're lying to me, Randy. I know what you and my husband have been up to for some time. Stealing little girls from their mommas and selling them to the prostitution rings back East and overseas. You disgust me." The gun in her hand began to tremble as Agnes, perhaps for the first time in a long time, became angry.

159

Emily noticed a shadow of fear, too, darken her eyes, and she guessed that it had ruled her adult life. Agnes had no doubt married very young, and this was probably the first time in her married life she had taken a stand.

"Now Agnes, just put the gun away. Hell, I bet you don't even know how to use the stupid thing. Come on now, let's talk about this, huh?" Taylor moved towards Agnes as if his towering figure would frighten her.

Agnes stepped out of the shadows. Teri gasped at the sight. Her mother's cheek swelled with a purple bruise.

"We'll talk." Agnes laughed without humor. The gun steadied in her hand and her voice chilled the air. "If you come one step closer to me, or if you ever touch me I'll kill you. Just like I killed John."

Taylor stopped in his tracks. He gulped, fear written across his face. There was a sparkle of insanity in Agnes's eyes. From somewhere in the distance, sirens screamed over the crackling thunder.

Teri and Emily went to the child who lay on the floor. She was so fragile and so tiny, Emily thought. At first she thought Gretchen was dead, then she saw her eyelids flutter.

"Am I dead?" Gretchen asked in a barely audible whisper.

With tears in her eyes, Teri smiled. "No, baby, you're safe with Mom now. Everything's going to be all right."

Gretchen closed her eyes and fell immediately to sleep.

CHAPTER THIRTEEN

When the police and the ambulance crews finally left the house, it was after midnight. Patricia drove Emily and Teri to the hospital, leaving Ashley, who refused medical attention, and Catherine alone in the house.

"Well, I guess that about wraps up the whole thing, doesn't it?" Ashley sighed as they stood on the porch watching the rain fall softly in the darkness that enveloped the old mansion.

Catherine thought for a moment. She shivered at the memory of Agnes Dupree with a gun in her hand. Blood had dotted her white sweater and Catherine wondered if the blood was hers or John Dupree's. Later, as Agnes gave her statement to the police, Catherine overheard what had happened earlier in the evening.

According to Agnes, she had suspected her husband for some time. At first, she thought that he was having an affair with another woman and that was what took him out of town frequently. And then, as the days stretched into months, the strange phone calls began coming in. That was when she began to see inexplicable long-distance phone charges to the East Coast — calls that had been made at all hours of the day and night.

"The clincher," she said, "was when John came up with enough money to buy this old place and have all of the work done on it."

The officer nodded politely as he scribbled notes on a pad.

"I confronted John about it this evening when I listened in on one of his long-distance calls to his friends back East. Needless to say, he beat the hell out of me and left me for dead. That was when I heard him call Taylor and learned about Gretchen. You know, I wondered why he raised such a fuss about hiring a team of experts to come in and investigate the hauntings here. It was actually me that wrote that letter to Madame Mistorie. After all was said and done, I guess he decided he'd best go along with it." Agnes grunted, a smile touching her lips.

There was no humor in her eyes, Catherine saw, only a deep sadness.

"I don't know how he could have done that with

my precious Gretchen." Her wet eyes pleaded with the officer as Teri squeezed her mother's hand. "I guess what you want to hear is, yes, I killed my husband, John Dupree."

After a few more questions, the officer gently lead Agnes to the waiting squad car and drove away. Teri stood motionless in the doorway and stared helplessly into the rain. Emily took Teri by the hand and led her out to the car. Catherine had watched them drive away, wondering to herself about the as-yet-unanswered questions.

Ashley said, "What are you thinking about?"

Catherine shrugged. "I feel sorry and sad that it all had to end this way. Poor Teri, can you imagine?"

Ashley took a moment to answer. "Things just come out the way they're supposed to, I guess."

"I just have this feeling of things being unfinished. Like, there are still parts of the story that we didn't find out."

"Like what?"

"Well, like, what happened to Rebecca? Was she really the poor soul left in the cellar with Charles? I just can't believe that Rebecca met her death in the cellar. So who was down there? And why weren't the bodies ever found? Could Emily's suspicions be true that you and Pat are somehow related to the Winslows?" At length, she shrugged her shoulders. Maybe we'll never know."

Catherine stepped into the house and made her way slowly to the parlor. Though she was very weary, she felt too wound up to retire. She caught a glimpse of the journal that she had left behind earlier, and she remembered that she hadn't finished reading it.

Ashley came in just as Catherine opened the book

to read the final page. Upon examination of the page, Catherine noticed that another hand had written the final words of the journal, and she began to read aloud.

July 23, 1896

Last night, the missus died in my arms. The Lord called her home and her pain is over. I will say nothing of that night other than Mister kilt her with his own hands.

Me and Rebecca dragged the body of Mister out to the fruit cellar and walled him in to keep his evil spirit there forever. We put crosses of the Lord around the walls and laid a Holy Bible at the back wall so he may never cross there. I carried the missus in my arms down to the cellar as was her dying wish. I laid her there in her best dressing gown with her rosary and her Bible. She said she was going to watch over him for eternity to keep him from hurting anyone else. I threw dirt over the doors to the fruit cellar and covered it with greenery so no one would suspect.

The missus told me of a letter she had written to her sister in the East in case something ever happened to her. I have never read the letter, but the missus says that her sister will know what was in her heart when she wrote it. Her sister's name is Windlow and I reckon that Rebecca and her child will change their name to protect the baby from the evils of her father's name.

I pray to the Lord Jesus that someone, someday, will find the terrible truths of what happened here, though I suspect that all will soon fall into ruins and only the spirits of those who lived here will walk as there is no rest for them.

Rinee

Ashley sighed. Her head was swimming. The past week seemed almost like a nightmare to her. "No wonder the daughters in the Windlow line have been haunted by the dreams for so long. You know, none of us ever had a clue. Our ancestors have always been shrouded with mystery and doubt. Now I know why. There are only so many things that a person can make up to cover the lies and the secrets. What happened here astounds me, and I can safely say I'm not proud of my past."

Catherine touched her arm.

Ashley shrugged, " I feel strangely liberated."

EPILOGUE

Gretchen spent a total of two weeks in the hospital. For the first couple of days she balanced on a thin and quavering line of life and death. When she showed signs of improvement, Emily and Teri decided to move Teri to Portland, and they began packing.

There was no trial for Randy Taylor. With all of the evidence pointing overwhelmingly to his guilt, and under the advice of his lawyer, he pleaded guilty and was sentenced to twenty years in prison.

With the return of her daughter, Teri opened a

new door toward improving her relationship with her mother. The first few meetings were painful but healing for all of them. She knew in time her mother would come to love Emily and her bizarre non-Christian ways as much as Teri did.

Emily returned to her little hole-in-the-wall shop with a renewed belief in herself. Her experiences with the Winslow house woke something deep within her. She felt more alive than she had for quite some time. A few weeks after her return, Emily made new flyers and repainted her front window. Along with all of her other talents, she added, "Psychic Investigator: Specialist in *All* Cases of Psychic Phenomena."

Patricia agreed to hang the flyer in her store despite Ashley's objections. In her heart she knew that what had happened at the Winslow mansion had changed all of them. Patricia found herself bored with everyday life. Without the thrill of not knowing what was going to happen next, without the fear that she honed her psychic abilities on, she felt as though she had lost something, and wondered what she did before she went to the mansion.

She contemplated writing a book about her experiences in Astoria, but each time she sat down at Marshal's old typewriter to start, words escaped her. She promised herself that someday she'd do it.

Ashley felt strangely different — more alive, attuned to the world. She began reading some of the books that crossed the counter at the store with a different eye. She had not seen Catherine since the day they left the mansion. She knew that Emily and Patricia still kept in contact with her, but Ashley refused to bend her pride enough to find out if Catherine married the fellow she was engaged to.

Sometimes late at night, she would wake from a sweet and pleasant dream about Catherine. She would lie there in the dark and smile. She knew she'd have to let her go soon, but she found it hard to open her hands to let the bird fly away from her.

One evening, a few months after the women had all returned back to their assorted workaday lives, Patricia asked Ashley if she would like to get in on another scheme that Emily had managed to drum up through her fliers. Ashley was not amused. But after a moment asked casually, "Is Catherine going to be in on this?"

Patricia smiled knowingly. "I believe Emily said she had included all of us in on the adventure. So I would say yes, she'll probably be there."

Ashley shrugged. "When are you all going to meet?"

"Tonight at my house."

Ashley chuckled. Patricia was trying to act as though she didn't know why Ashley had had a change of heart.

"I'll be there, I guess." Ashley pulled a set of keys out of her pocket.

"Tonight at seven," Patricia said as Ashley swung the door open and stepped out into the street.

Ashley waved and disappeared into the darkness.

Ashley tried hard not to stare at Catherine as the five of them gathered in Patricia's sitting room for coffee and dessert. She couldn't help but notice that

Catherine wasn't wearing a wedding band — but maybe she hadn't wanted one of those either. Still, her hopes burned inside her.

Distracted by her own thoughts, she only half heard what Emily was saying. It wasn't until the women stood and stretched their legs, that Ashley snapped out of it.

"Ashley, were you even listening to anything I said all night? It's very important that everyone knows what's going on before we load up and go." Emily crossed her arms and tried to look angry.

Ashley smiled slightly. "I guess I'm just really tired. I think I'll step out for some air, and then I promise I'll be wide awake and you'll have my full attention."

Emily nodded. "I think all of us could use a breath of fresh air. Mind if I join you?"

Ashley glanced at Catherine, and something stirred inside her. "No, not at all."

Emily and Teri intentionally slowed down and stopped as the group walked. Patricia had opted to stay in. She wanted to look at some books on witches before the group plunged into their next project.

Ashley couldn't stand the silence — or the million questions that whizzed around her head — any longer. She wished that her words sounded stronger than they did when she asked, "I imagine you're married now, aren't you?"

Catherine smiled. "Haven't you been talking with your mother and Emily? I called the whole thing off. My mother threw such a big fit that she disinherited me. She claimed I was not her daughter. Her daughter was dead to her. I've been living with Patricia until I can get out on my own again. She's been so kind to me."

Ashley stopped in her tracks. Shyly, she met Catherine's eyes. "What did you do that was so bad that your mother would disinherit you?"

Catherine laughed. "What makes you think that I did anything wrong?" Ashley shrugged and was about to speak when Catherine continued soberly, "I told her I was in love with someone else, not the man she'd picked out for me. I told her I loved you."

Ashley felt her knees grow weak. She smiled shakily. "Why didn't you call me?"

Catherine shrugged, "Why didn't you call me? I guess I thought that . . ."

Ashley pulled Catherine to her. Softly, they kissed. Ashley's heart was thumping so hard she feared that it would stop suddenly under the stress.

Down the walkway Emily smiled to herself. From the moment she saw Catherine she knew that she and Ashley were bound to be together. It was fate. And she had seen it in the cards. She just hoped that this new turn of events wouldn't stop the investigation she had lined up in Sachet, Idaho. She had already accepted half her fee from a woman who claimed to be the headmistress of an all-girls school there. A woman who claimed her school was plagued by a coven of black witches.

A few of the publications of
THE NAIAD PRESS, INC.
P.O. Box 10543 • Tallahassee, Florida 32302
Phone (904) 539-5965
Toll-Free Order Number: 1-800-533-1973
Mail orders welcome. Please include 15% postage.

FOREVER by Evelyn Kennedy. 224 pp. Passionate romance — love
overcoming all obstacles.   ISBN 1-56280-094-9 $10.95

WHISPERS by Kris Bruyer. 176 pp. Romantic ghost story
                                    ISBN 1-56280-082-5   10.95

NIGHT SONGS by Penny Mickelbury. 224 pp. A Gianna
Maglione Mystery. Second in a series. ISBN 1-56280-097-3   10.95

GETTING TO THE POINT by Teresa Stores. 256 pp. Classic
southern Lesbian novel.   ISBN 1-56280-100-7   10.95

PAINTED MOON by Karin Kallmaker. 224 pp. Delicious
Kallmaker romance.   ISBN 1-56280-075-2   9.95

THE MYSTERIOUS NAIAD edited by Katherine V. Forrest &
Barbara Grier. 320 pp. Love stories by Naiad Press authors.
                                    ISBN 1-56280-074-4   14.95

DAUGHTERS OF A CORAL DAWN by Katherine V. Forrest.
240 pp. Tenth Anniversay Edition.   ISBN 1-56280-104-X   10.95

BODY GUARD by Claire McNab. 208 pp. A Carol Ashton Mystery.
6th in a series.   ISBN 1-56280-073-6   9.95

CACTUS LOVE by Lee Lynch. 192 pp. Stories by the beloved
storyteller.   ISBN 1-56280-071-X   9.95

SECOND GUESS by Rose Beecham. 216 pp. An Amanda Valentine
Mystery. 2nd in a series.   ISBN 1-56280-069-8   9.95

THE SURE THING by Melissa Hartman. 208 pp. L.A. earthquake
romance.   ISBN 1-56280-078-7   9.95

A RAGE OF MAIDENS by Lauren Wright Douglas. 240 pp. A
Caitlin Reece Mystery. 6th in a series. ISBN 1-56280-068-X   9.95

TRIPLE EXPOSURE by Jackie Calhoun. 224 pp. Romantic drama
involving many characters.   ISBN 1-56280-067-1   9.95

UP, UP AND AWAY by Catherine Ennis. 192 pp. Delightful
romance.   ISBN 1-56280-065-5   9.95

PERSONAL ADS by Robbi Sommers. 176 pp. Sizzling short
stories.   ISBN 1-56280-059-0   9.95

FLASHPOINT by Katherine V. Forrest. 256 pp. Lesbian
blockbuster! ISBN 1-56280-043-4 22.95

CROSSWORDS by Penny Sumner. 256 pp. 2nd Victoria Cross
Mystery. ISBN 1-56280-064-7 9.95

SWEET CHERRY WINE by Carol Schmidt. 224 pp. A novel of
suspense. ISBN 1-56280-063-9 9.95

CERTAIN SMILES by Dorothy Tell. 160 pp. Erotic short stories.
ISBN 1-56280-066-3 9.95

EDITED OUT by Lisa Haddock. 224 pp. 1st Carmen Ramirez
Mystery. ISBN 1-56280-077-9 9.95

WEDNESDAY NIGHTS by Camarin Grae. 288 pp. Sexy
adventure. ISBN 1-56280-060-4 10.95

SMOKEY O by Celia Cohen. 176 pp. Relationships on the
playing field. ISBN 1-56280-057-4 9.95

KATHLEEN O'DONALD by Penny Hayes. 256 pp. Rose and
Kathleen find each other and employment in 1909 NYC.
ISBN 1-56280-070-1 9.95

STAYING HOME by Elisabeth Nonas. 256 pp. Molly and Alix
want a baby . . . or do they? ISBN 1-56280-076-0 10.95

TRUE LOVE by Jennifer Fulton. 240 pp. Six lesbians searching
for love in all the "right" places. ISBN 1-56280-035-3 9.95

GARDENIAS WHERE THERE ARE NONE by Molleen Zanger.
176 pp. Why is Melanie inextricably drawn to the old house?
ISBN 1-56280-056-6 9.95

KEEPING SECRETS by Penny Mickelbury. 208 pp. A Gianna
Maglione Mystery. First in a series. ISBN 1-56280-052-3 9.95

THE ROMANTIC NAIAD edited by Katherine V. Forrest &
Barbara Grier. 336 pp. Love stories by Naiad Press authors.
ISBN 1-56280-054-X 14.95

UNDER MY SKIN by Jaye Maiman. 336 pp. A Robin Miller
mystery. 3rd in a series. ISBN 1-56280-049-3. 10.95

STAY TOONED by Rhonda Dicksion. 144 pp. Cartoons — 1st
collection since *Lesbian Survival Manual.* ISBN 1-56280-045-0 9.95

CAR POOL by Karin Kallmaker. 272pp. Lesbians on wheels
and then some! ISBN 1-56280-048-5 9.95

These are just a few of the many Naiad Press titles. — we are the oldest and
largest lesbian/feminist publishing company in the world. Please request a
complete catalog. We offer personal service; we encourage and welcome
direct mail orders from individuals who have limited access to bookstores
carrying our publications.